KARISMA TROUBLE

An
Unfortunate
Lineage

VOLUME
III

A Novella

KARISMA
TROUBLE

An
Unfortunate
Lineage

VOLUME
III

A Novella

Delaine Christine

Karisma Trouble
An Unfortunate Lineage Volume III

ISBN-13: 978-1950563111

Copyright © by Delaine Christine 2020

Original Publication 2016 as Tortured #1 RavenCroft Series. Re-
Published in 2018:as Trouble: Narrated by Vortigern Black, The
RavenCroft Saga

Book and Book Cover Design by DC Johnson
Model Pic by Marcelo Krelling, used with permission
Scenic Cover Image by andreiuc88 via 123rf.com
Interior Model Image by Badmanproduction, used with permission

Kimerah Publishing, Elkhart, IN

Printed in the United States of America.

The Prophecy
Continues...

Through waxen hair no gift doth breed
for surely lacking the strength of seed.

Another shall come on the last of day.
A writer's word shows another way.

PROLOGUE

Vortigern Black here.
That's right, I'm Baaaack!

Did you miss me?

Seriously ... didn't you miss me? I've been gone for a whole book after all! Well, almost anyway. Then again, maybe you don't know that yet. Maybe this is the first you've heard of me.

In which case, if you have arrived here first without reading the other two volumes that precede it then you might want to consider backing up because you **will** miss out on a **lot** if you don't.

If you are a returning fan of mine looking for more clues as to which character within this story I, Vortigern Black am, then I assure you, you will not be disappointed. If you're not a returning fan and are new to all of this then welcome dear reader to the An Unfortunate Lineage series!

To start, in order to make this introduction as concise, quick, and painless as possible, I have made a list of points to cover with you, the reader.

The author of this here tale, you know, Ms. Christine... Well, she argued with me over whether such a list was necessary. She thinks readers are smarter than I give them credit for.

But I disagree.

Oh, I don't mean that you're not smart. I bet you have all kinds of education, degrees, and general common sense going on in those heads of yours. No, what I mean is, I think lists are very important and since the introduction is my responsibility, I get to do whatever I want to, within it.

Hehehe.

And so, without further ado...

By the end of volume two, Kayos Effect we learned that...

-One, Lionel Radford, a very naughty drug lord and the former husband of Sable RavenCroft, aka Kalysta Radford, has been shot and killed by Astraia O'Kahner's late husband, during an under-cover op and drug exchange that he intentionally got in the middle of. The stupid and irresponsible action got him killed and...

-Two, put his family at risk. So now, Astraia O'Kahner and her children are in extreme danger of being murdered by Kobi Radford's henchmen. They were to be placed in a safehouse with Agents Pegueros and Kastle until they could be relocated to a new Witness Protection Location. That's right, the very same one with the leak mentioned in volume one. Those familiar with the first volume might also recall Agent Pegueros had been working under-cover within the Radford's drug cartel and that he had a hand in assisting in Sable's escape from her violent estranged husband. Unfortunately...

-Three, it turns out there is no place safe for Astraia and her kids within the United States, accept one. Okay, actually there are two but the Blackthorne's don't know about the RavenCroft's yet. They are aware, however, that...

-Four, Astraia O'Kahner became Alaina Jordan and married Dante Blackthorne, aka Franc Kastle. The couple are now happily expecting triplets in the next seven to eight months. And yes, I know what you all are thinking... Enough with the excessive name changes already, right? Because they're highly annoying. Sheesh! That's about as annoying as...

-Five, learning there is a prophecy which may well link both the RavenCroft's and the Blackthorne's by more than just blood and an extensive lineage. But that doesn't hold a candle to learning from an angel, of all things...

-Six, that trouble is brewing in Loveland, Colorado, which is why we are returning to cover more of the RavenCroft's story now.

Whewie!

That's a lot in and of itself, and the fact that Sable RavenCroft has been officially widowed by Alaina's late husband might seem like a good thing for her to some readers, but I'm not too sure that's the case.

The thing is, the RavenCroft's don't know Lionel is dead yet, and though Sable may no longer have to worry about him once she does find out, it by no means lessens the danger she now faces from her former brother-in-law, Kobi Radford, for...

-One, he is madder than you can imagine over his

brother's death, and as stated previously, out for blood because...

-Two, he knows his former sister-in-law is **not** dead and…

-Three, he found out it was all a ruse for her to escape with her kids. The problem is, he thinks Sable took off with proof of both the Radford's drug trafficking as well as the identity of a high-ranking mole within the CIA, which Kobi happens to have in his back pocket. The very same official who made him aware of the subterfuge in the first place. The truth is, she only had in her possession proof of the mole because Agent Pegueros disappeared with the flash drive that had all the drug trafficking information on it. That was handed over to Agent Jericho Henley, his supervisor.

Here's a little something neither the RavenCroft's nor the Blackthorne's know yet, and I only do because of the notes of the original author that I'm privy to.

Kobi thinks Alaina is Sable and that the man who killed his brother was a man Sable hired to take him out.

Well, there's a mess for you.

Would you believe life among the RavenCroft's is about to get messier?

The thing is, Kahner and Sable RavenCroft and Dante and Alaina Blackthorne aren't alone in this vast tale. Though there is more to both of these couples stories we will not be covering that in this volume. No indeed, but now that we have you all up to speed it's time to switch gears on you.

Annoying, yes, but necessary, nonetheless.

This particular story you have in your hands today

is filled with all kinds of trouble, hence the title. It could also be considered a dark romance for it tells the story of Kalabernus RavenCroft. He is the second born of a set of triplets and has an ability that is more like a curse. His father, Bastion RavenCroft would argue otherwise but I say…

Not!

Hello! The man has been seeing shadowy demon-like creatures of whom have been tormenting him since he was a child. Sound familiar? Kind of like his cousin, Drinian Blackthorne from the last volume, eh? You sure as heck aren't going to convince me that seeing and hearing those nasty creatures is a blessing.

Kalabernus's story starts in Loveland, Colorado and, like in the tale of his brother, Kahner, it began fifteen years ago only a month later, in November. Yes, the year two thousand does seem to be ending with some upsetting events for the RavenCrofts. Just last month Kalabernus's brother, Kahner, divorced his first wife and was taking the breakup pretty hard. And now this month…

Well, just read, you'll see.

Don't really think this one needs a lead in. This story of trouble and woe, sort of tells it all.

I should warn you though, you may well be gaining more than just Kalabernus's perspective on the events that transpire.

Chapter 1

"You're a bit terrifying sometimes. You know that, right?"

Shifting uneasily in the driver's seat, Kalabernus RavenCroft's crystal-clear blue eyes shimmered within the dark car in distress.

"I'm sorry, Stacey. I don't mean to be," he responded urgently, not wanting to frighten her. He peered over at the pretty young woman at his side. At twenty-five years of age, he had finally gone on his first date ever, with a real live girl, and he didn't want to ruin it. When she'd said yes to his date proposal he'd been dumbfounded. Most women ran from him out of fear, but Stacey Lynn was different.

"I don't mind. Really, I don't," she said sweetly even as her eyes darted anxiously about her.

He could see her shiver almost violently and knew it hadn't been from being cold. The heater was on high and warmth flooded the car.

Kalabernus scowled.

Silently he urged the shadows to stop messing with her. The moment he started talking to them to get them to stop he knew he'd lose his chance with her. But they were messing with her bad, and it was angering him.

Two of the troublesome three were swirling around her right before his very eyes, their inky cloud like essences were heckling him gleefully. He knew what they were trying to do. They were attempting to frighten Stacey away, which is what they'd done with every woman he'd ever expressed interest in.

Kalabernus's beefy hands tightened on the steering wheel angrily as he swore silently. Why couldn't the shadows just leave him alone?

"Did you enjoy the movie?" He swatted his enormous hand toward Veranke. The inky black creature slithered towards her through the window of the car, joining his cohorts. Stacey jumped, not for the first time baffled by her date's odd behavior.

"S...sorry." Kalabernus stammered, "didn't mean to frighten you," He quickly jerked his hand back. The troublesome three were now at full strength with Veranke present. Their greenish-black substance seemed to fill the empty space between them making it hard to see out the passenger window.

"You didn't, but it's starting to rain so you might want to watch the road." Stacey smiled easily and calmly gestured toward the street in front of her.

"Right, of course." He turned his head away. She looked so pretty; he couldn't help but stare. Catching a flash of light out of the corner of his eye, Kalabernus heard the rumble of a thunderstorm coming in the distance. A smattering of tiny water droplets plopped against his windshield - a prelude of the deluge to come.

"Better get you home before it starts pouring," he said, enjoying the easy smile she directed his way. He grinned, and his heart thudded fiercely in his chest at the notion of a first kiss.

He'd never kissed a woman before either.

In unison, the troublesome three unexpectedly began screeching in a loud crescendo, forcing Kalabernus to cover his ears. Cringing painfully at the sound and the terrifying sight of their blood red eyes glowing with menace, he couldn't help but shut his own eyes. Whimpering shamefully in distress, he missed seeing the driver speeding toward the town intersection, which had been the demon's intent.

Kalabernus was unable to careen out of the way.

The darkness seemed to envelop the two individuals within the vehicle as a multitude of eerie evil cries resounded in his ears. Their worlds began to spin as the car flipped from the impact. The sound of screeching, grinding metal upon pavement was the only thing discernable through his otherwise darkened senses. The feeling of weightlessness, as though flying through the air left him disoriented and unaware of the inevitable impact.

Lightning struck nearby as thunder boomed across the city of Loveland, bringing him back to a semi-conscious state mere seconds later. Fragmented sections of light blanketed the sky. An explosion of sound reverberated across the expansive distant mountainside as Kalabernus suddenly erupted in a panic from the sidewalk where he'd been thrown. Ignoring the jarring pain from having hit the hard ground with such force he refused to acknowledge any discomfort existed. He stumbled as he ran, his vision blurring from blood dripping down his forehead. There were jagged cuts from broken glass covering his face and arms and a nasty bump on his head.

Nipping at his heels as they slithered behind him were the ethereal black forms of his tormentors who were always ever present at his side. They cackled in their triumph, circling him as he attempted to run toward the vehicle, whipping around him effortlessly as though in a ritualistic dance of sorts. Normally his body would jerk in place and he'd fall to his knees in a malleable mess but not this time. The panic within him surged, his heart pounding wildly in his vast chest as the determination to save Stacey overcame his fear of the shadows.

Skidding to a halt several feet from the vehicle, which had flipped over and now sat roof first on the pavement, Kalabernus roared in distress.

"Stacey, nooooo!"

Heart filled with dread at the sight before him, Kalabernus could see her small form was pinned beneath the roof of the car.

Cackling at his ear, the demons Veranke and Zalman taunted him further.

"Dead. Ha! Smashed like a little dolly," Veranke shouted with glee. His oily black vaporous form slithered about Kalabernus, attempting to dissuade him from further movement. "Shame on you."

"Not paying attention," Fallen accused while screaming in his ear.

"Murderer! Tsk, tsk, tsk." Zalman snarled with a devilish eerie grin.

"Get away from me." Kalabernus punched through Veranke's form as though he were a mere wisp of smoke. He charged toward the vehicle as people began descending upon the street from the neighboring restaurants and bar, having heard the accident occur.

Kalabernus frantically attempted to determine the best way to get the car off of Stacey. Tears splattered down his cheeks and his face was wrought with tortured emotion. Scrambling around the vehicle, he tried to determine his best leverage point.

"Off! Gotta get it off!" Yelling in a panic, his voice boomed across the street as he sobbed. The onlookers shrunk away, a few pulling out cell phones to call for help even as sirens could be heard in the distance.

Bending down next to Stacey where she lay, he struggled for a handhold, scraping his fingers on the pavement painfully. Leveraging his body weight, Kalabernus shoved at the car door with his brute strength, causing it to rock and lift slightly, just enough to allow for him to reach under the roof of the car. Taking a firm hold, he groaned and growled, his face contorting from the exertion he was extolling, his jaw clenching as he bit down hard with his teeth. The jagged edge of the roof bit into his hand, cutting him, but he could no longer feel any pain.

Praying, that if there was a God that He'd allow him to lift the car away from the woman pinned below it, Kalabernus heaved with all his might, roaring from the strain. Venting one last guttural cry, he bounced with his knees in his crouched state, then flung the car with such force that it flipped over and landed back onto the roof of the car. It skidded to a halt near the streetlight.

Oblivious to the shocked, terrified gazes of the pedestrians, Kalabernus bent down toward Stacey's prone form on the ground. The fact he'd just punted a car across the street as though it were a toy was lost on him, as he took in the pallor of her complexion. It was ghostly white, and blood was oozing from her waist where the car had her pinned. Afraid to move her, for fear she might be paralyzed, Kalabernus ripped off his shirt, wadded it up, and pressed it against her waist.

When the emergency vehicles and police cars pulled up seconds later it was to the sight of an eerily quiet crowd and the giant of a man sobbing uncontrollably over a woman lying in the street.

Mumbling incoherently about vengeance and demonic shadows, Kalabernus had to be forcefully pulled away by half a dozen cops and two firemen. Leaning over Stacey the first paramedic grimaced as he tried to feel for a pulse. After making several attempts to jump-start her heart, they finally gave voice to what they'd known when they'd first arrived at the scene.

"Time of death," the paramedic said quietly, closing the young woman's pretty brown eyes. "Ten thirty-seven."

"No. No, no, Stacey!" Kalabernus hollered. The shadows in the street, of whom only he could see began whirling about as though in a gleeful dance. More had converged upon the street as the paramedics and officers had worked. Their hazy greenish black forms twisted and gyrated in a grotesque fashion. They mocked Kalabernus and hindered the many officers from working the scene in order to assist the other driver. Their blood red eyes gleamed in satisfaction at the reaction they were instilling within him as they tripped people, caused them to fumble, or distracted them with other matters by whispering in their ears.

"Stop it, all of you. You blasted cursed demons! How dare you? How could you do this?" Kalabernus shouted. Running about the street he punched at the air, looking like a wild man who had gone crazy from drink.

"You wretched, vile creatures. *You did this,*" he roared. "*You caused this to happen!*" Kalabernus swung around suddenly, arms swiping through their shapeless forms as they dissipated and reappeared behind him. He was unaware of the frightening, even terrifying spectacle he was creating for those watching from the street who couldn't see what he could.

"How could you? She was all I had," he shouted, his voice echoing in the night as he spun around, his haunting blue eyes flashing brightly in the dim streetlights. His short black hair clung to his head from the blood dripping off his forehead from his own injuries.

"Did you lose your friend?" The shadow Fallon wheezed, twisting itself into the form of a man without a clear face.

"*We?*" Veranke mocked next to Fallen, taking a similar form. "Why would we care for *her?* Why would *we…?*" They laughed evilly as Kalabernus lashed out at them enraged and disgusted by their callousness, not caring what kind of scene he might be making.

They wrapped around him then, taking leave of their human forms as they slithered about him. Head bowed Kalabernus's shoulders slumped in defeat. He cried out at the night sky, hopelessness overwhelming him. Shaking his head as the rain erupted from the sky and began to pour down upon him in torrents he glared back at Stacey's lifeless body then slumped to the ground with a tortured cry.

Arriving at the scene of the accident Bastion RavenCroft emerged from his son's Deputy Sheriff's cruiser. Seeing first the sheet-covered body on the ground he turned in alarm toward the sound of a wounded animal wailing into the night. Kalabernus's vast shirtless frame was bent over on the ground. His haunted, pain-filled, bloody expression filled in the blanks without the need for questions. Troubled by the scene before him, he moved purposefully toward his son only to be stopped.

"Wait, Dad. You need to hear this." Kalturek halted his movements.

"Not now, Kalturek. Your brother needs me," Bastion declared heatedly, attempting to move past him.

"No, Dad, stop! Just listen," Kalturek insisted, guiding the figure next to him closer to his father so he could hear.

Irritated Bastion scowled. "What is it then?"

Sniffling as she sobbed the young woman before him appeared both frightened and in awe as she spoke. "He lifted it off of her."

"Sorry?"

"Kalabernus, sir," Angela said quietly, anxious to be speaking with the RavenCroft patriarch in person. The man made for a formidable sight himself in his black Stetson and duster. "I think he was trying to save her. He... well, he just lifted the car up off of her and threw it over there. "

Pointing toward the mangled vehicle butting up against the stoplight Bastion's gaze followed the direction of her arm. Startled by what she said Bastion recognized the woman and realized she'd gone to school with his sons as well as Stacey.

"Did he really?" Bastion was astonished. She nodded, and his gaze shifted toward Kalabernus where he knelt in the street. He had always been a giant among men, but Bastion never imagined he'd be capable of such immense strength as to lift a car.

"It took eight men to get him away from her, so the paramedics could work." Emotion charged Kalturek's voice as he spoke.

An agonizing wail emitted from Kalabernus's throat, piercing the night air. Bastion grimaced then strode with purpose toward Kalabernus. At twenty-five years of age, Stacey Lynn had been his son's first crush, his first love, and his first and only date. Noting the frightened gazes of the many female onlookers who were shrinking away from the scene, Bastion had to acknowledge, at that moment, that Stacey had likely been his last.

Chapter 2

Mighty sad set of circumstances wouldn't you say? And Stacey Lynn was Kalabernus's last attempt at a romantic foray for a long, long time.

As was the case in the previous book, this one also jumps forward nearly fifteen years. It is now November of two thousand fifteen. We're still in Loveland, Colorado and will continue on in this location for the rest of this story.

During the span of fifteen years, Kalabernus becomes something of a recluse. Though college-educated, much of it was completed from home where possible and, his career path took a decidedly different one from the rest of his siblings. You see, Kalabernus, though clearly tormented by shadowy demonic creatures, is a highly gifted individual. His father, Bastion, discovered early on that his son excelled in music and was very good with his hands. Though more than capable of creating beautiful sculptures and working with wood, the area to which he excelled most was with painting, and he'd made quite a name for himself even on an international level.

For the most part, Kalabernus kept to himself. He rarely, if ever, came into town, preferring instead to stay within the protective enclosure of the Croft Haven raven sanctuary. There, he could work in peace within his studio above the garage at the RavenCroft horse ranch. He'd learned early on in life that people feared him just by being in his presence for not only did he have an unsettling aura about him, but he was extremely intimidating in size and stature. As a result, he had very little experience communicating with people, women in particular. Most of the time he was more than inclined to avoid contact with anyone. But sometimes on Fridays, when the shadows weren't bothering him too bad, he'd take himself into town to Shenanigans, his favorite local karaoke and dance bar for a drink. If he was in a really good mood, which was rare, he'd bless the crowd with a song or two.

Today, Kalabernus was in a really good mood, having learned several of his paintings would be displayed at the Denver Art Museum. So, he stopped into Shenanigans, took his favored seat at the bar, and ordered his usual.

- - -

Kalabernus had been watching from the bar for some time now. At first, because he'd been entranced by her beautiful face. But then mostly because Kalabernus realized that this very same person was an extremely curvaceous chestnut-haired beauty who was undressing in front of his very eyes.

Okay, maybe not undressing, but she was taking off her coat and for Kalabernus that was about as close to seeing a woman undressing as he was going to get. Trying not to stare or ogle her, he shifted his brooding gaze toward the girls singing karaoke across the room. But his full attention never wavered from the woman from the moment she'd entered the bar.

She was of medium build, but he noted rather tall in height. Observing her step around the table she was sitting down at with her girlfriend, Angela Hayes, he noted she was wearing three-inch heel boots which explained the height. Harrumphing softly at her subterfuge he wondered briefly why women wore such blasted precarious footwear. He couldn't imagine they were comfortable to walk in at all, though admittedly on her they were very appealing.

Cradling his beer, he noted her shoulders tense as she slid into her chair. Head peering cautiously about the room, her unusual almond shaped amber eyes locked onto his. Not accustomed to getting caught staring, he shifted uneasily then smiled weakly, giving her what he hoped appeared to be an appreciative nod.

"Angela, who is that?" Sareena Davis inquired of her friend upon catching the man eyeing her. The sensation of being watched was by no means unfamiliar to her. She suspected it would take time getting used to normal people casually observing her as opposed to a stalker. Tapping her hand on the table to get Angela's attention she shifted her head ever so slightly toward the bar, where the enormous man sat drinking his beer. She'd never seen a man quite so huge before and he was gorgeous too.

"Oh, you mean that marvelous piece of eye candy sitting at the bar?" Angela replied with a nervous giggle. "That would be Kalabernus RavenCroft. I went to school with him and his brothers Kalturek and Kahner. They're triplets."

Eyes widening Sareena gaped. "Triplets? Are they all as big as him?" she marveled. Trying to shift her gaze back to the bar in a way that she could see better, she regretted instantly not having sat in the opposite chair. Getting up and moving now though would be too obvious.

Laughing, Angela gestured for a waitress and grabbed the peanut bowl from the table, pushing it closer so they both could reach.

"Almost. He's the biggest of the three but the twins…"

"Did you say twins?"

"Oh, right. Yeah, I probably should warn you. Kalturek is one of them and he's the county Sheriff. And Kahner's the other. He just returned home from a tour with the U.S. army recently, with a new wife. They're identical so if you run into one of them…"

"Right, be sure I know who I'm saying 'hi' to if I meet them again. Thanks for the heads up."

Noting Sareena attempting another secretive glance his way Angela chuckled then thought better to make light.

"Listen, Sareena, where Kalabernus is concerned... With your past, you're likely going to want to stay clear."

"Why? Is he dangerous or something?" Sareena asked her curiosity morbidly peaked. She noted the man's brooding good looks and amazing crystal-clear blue eyes even from where she sat.

"Funny you ask whether he's dangerous first, rather than whether he's married."

"Oh, right, of course. Anyone who looks that good has got to be married."

Eager to correct her friend's inaccurate assumption Angela shook her head. "No, it's not that. He's single, it's just...."

"What can I get for you ladies?" the waitress asked, interrupting them. Placing their order, Sareena noted Angela conveniently steered the conversation to another topic and wondered at why. For the next half hour, they munched on appetizers while catching up on old times and listened to the brave souls within the karaoke bar who were courageous enough to take up the microphone. Some were mind-numbingly painful to listen to, many were amusing, and occasionally they were surprised by a few good ones.

After a while, they're heads both turned upon overhearing a commotion at the bar next to them. Three attractive men all sporting black hair and large builds had joined Kalabernus. They were boisterous, acting slightly drunk and appeared to be in good spirits. Two of them, Sareena observed, were identical in appearance.

"Those are his three brothers." Angela offered, seeing Sareena's curious gaze. She was amused by her friend's interest. "Drayke is the youngest and the smallest of the lot."

"He's considered small? That man has got to be easily six foot two or more and built to boot."

"Not sure but sounds about right. Kalabernus is six foot eight, though. Know that for a fact."

"How?"

"He told me once. One of those random conversations you never expect." Angela shrugged, observing her friend eyeing the men at the bar with a mixture of amusement and trepidation. "But they're all married, though."

"Except this Kalab guy?"

"Kalabernus," Angela corrected.

"That's an unusual name," Sareena commented off-handedly, her eyes shifting toward the bar where the man was being not so gently forced from his seat.

"It's really good to see that happy light in your face again. Especially after everything you went through with that stalker." Angela said, glancing almost worriedly at Kalabernus as he was being prompted loudly by his brothers to sing, then back at her friend.

"I don't want to think about that tonight," Sareena replied dismissively. "Besides, that was when I lived in Massachusetts and I'm in Colorado now. He can't get to me here," she said with relief, glad to be finally rid of the whole mess. She should have thought of this idea a long time ago. Maybe then she could have saved herself some pain and, for that matter, her friend Kami's life.

Feeling a sudden jolt from behind, Sareena careened forward in her seat, knocking over her wine cooler. Head turning to see what or who had bumped her, she saw one of the RavenCroft brothers had fallen into her, as he was attempting to force his brother up to the stage.

"Sorry about that," Drayke called jovially, stepping away from her. Doing a double take at the sight of Sareena, he whistled softly and gave her a winning smile. "Dang, honey, you're a mighty fine-looking woman." The words slipped out before he could stop them.

His response elicited a giggle as Sareena flushed with heat.

"Careful, Drayke. You want your wife catching you talking like that?" Kalturek chided with a disgusted shake of his head. His brother was always such a flirt and it often got him in trouble with his wife, Laynie.

Tired of being manhandled Kalabernus shrugged off his brother's arms irately, embarrassed by the attention he was getting. Angela and her friend with soft amber eyes and delicate china doll features were staring at him, and he was having trouble thinking through the beer and the mesmerizing gray eyes.

"Just get off of me!" Kalabernus exclaimed. "S...sorry about my brothers," he stammered toward Sareena, wishing he didn't sound like a blubbering idiot. "Are you all right?" he asked urgently. "Drayke didn't hurt you, did he? Cause if he did I'll clobber him for you," he said darkly, turning swiftly on his brother who reflexively backed away.

Sareena's face lit up and her gray eyes twinkled merrily at his genuine concern. Though brutish in size and stature he was clearly a teddy bear at heart. Placing her hand gently on his arm, she stopped him from striking at Drayke.

Kalabernus turned back toward her in surprise.

"It's okay, really. I'm okay." Sareena crooned sweetly, staring up into his pale blue eyes. Their conversation garnered the attention of his brothers who exchanged interested glances. Women didn't talk to their brother, regardless of his exceptional good looks. They were usually too afraid to get near him because of the dark presence he exuded.

"Well, okay then," Kalabernus said softly, his voice low and smooth. "But if you change your mind…"

Sareena laughed, the genuinely delighted sound garnering a sharp intake of breath from Kalabernus at the sound. "I won't, Kalabernus, but thanks," she said softly, startling him.

"How do you know my name? Because I would remember you if I'd met you." Kalabernus asked urgently. He glanced toward Angela suspiciously who rolled her eyes and peered quickly away, a look of embarrassment on her own face. Clearly, they'd been talking about him, he realized, and he could only imagine what Angela was saying.

Heat infused Sareena's cheeks as she blushed again. She was fully aware his brother's eyes were intently watching the exchange for some reason, appearing almost anxious.

"I felt your eyes upon me, so I figured I'd better find out who you were," Sareena stated, attempting to turn things around on him.

Looking for something, anything to distract him from her sensual lips Kalabernus glanced toward the table and noticed her spilled drink.

"He spilled your drink. I'll make him buy you a new one." Kalabernus shoved his brother toward the bar. "Buy her a new drink, Drayke," he demanded with a scowl. "It's the least you can do for bumping her and spilling her drink while manhandling me."

Chuckling, Drayke eyed the woman mischievously then Kalabernus. "Fine, but only if you sing."

"All right." Kalabernus agreed with an exasperated growl. "But I get to choose. None of that namby-pamby drivel you guys are always trying to get me to sing." Adjusting his belt buckle self-consciously, he strolled to the stage. The crowd within the pub erupted in excited applause.

"Oh, my! You are in for a rare treat tonight," Angela stated. Seeing her friends questioning look she chuckled. "Just wait, you'll see. Wonder what he's going to choose tonight?"

"Here you go. Sorry for the trouble." Drayke said, at Sareena's side. Wine cooler in hand, she noticed he was about to open it for her.

"No! I got it, thanks." Sareena said quickly, grabbing the bottle from Drayke's grasp. Seeing his questioning look she apologized. "Sorry. No offense intended. I just make it a practice not to accept opened drinks from people," she explained apologetically.

Drayke gave her a calculating stare, somehow suspecting the woman had a good reason for her statement. "Good practice to keep." Acknowledging Angela with a cursory nod he walked away.

Moments later the beginning music score of Lee Brice's song, Drinking Class filled the air to the delight of the crowd. Chairs could be heard scooting about as people attempted to get a better vantage for the performance. Though well known by all for his brooding and frightening visage Kalabernus was also well known for his talented voice.

The RavenCroft brothers heckled from the bar while leaning against it, beers in hand.

"Yeah!" Kahner yelled across the crowd, enjoying the chance to hear his brother sing for the first time since he had returned home. He'd been away working undercover with the CIA for nearly fifteen years and was grateful for Kalturek's suggestion that they all go out. It had been a long time and Kahner had been cooped up at the ranch for the past couple of weeks.

Kalabernus began singing, surprising Sareena at the quality of his voice. Smooth and deep with just the right amount of edge, his vocals suited the song perfectly. Belting it out as though he'd been singing professionally for years, he soon had the crowd on their feet shaking their drinks and singing along with him. Being as it was Friday night the song seemed to resonate with nearly everyone after a long work week.

Sareena simply couldn't take her eyes off him, and she noticed his gaze flit her way a few times as he sang. It had been several years since she'd been able to feel such freedom as she was now. Secure in the knowledge that she no longer had to worry about her stalker she found she was enjoying herself. Smiling dreamily and laughing with delight as Kalabernus finished the song, the crowd erupted in raucous applause and hooting. Shortly after, his brothers joined him on stage and all four men belted out another country song together, all the while playing it up with bad grammar and many antics.

Several singers and songs later, the karaoke machine was put away, and the band for the night began to play. The dance floor opened, and people began moving out onto the floor as more people began pouring into the bar for the dance phase of the night.

Sareena excused herself to the restroom and Angela opted to join her. Returning to their table Sareena picked up her third wine cooler of the night figuring it would be her last. Noticing it was full she didn't really think too much of it. She had a weakness for wine coolers because they tasted so much better than beer, so she usually limited herself to no more than three.

Her thoughts kept returning to Kalabernus who was sitting alone at the bar. He was something of a paradox to her. Being as attractive as he was in addition to a talented singer, who was clearly able to engage those around him when he sang, she would have thought he'd have women clamoring all over him.

Instead, he appeared to be a loner. More than that, people within the bar seemed to give him a wide birth. The bar was clearly crowded for the night, not a seat empty other than the table right next to him as well as the two bar stools on either side of him.

Caught up in her musings Sareena managed to finish off her wine cooler before she realized it. She was feeling especially good for some reason tonight after finishing the third one. Noting Angela was busy flirting with one of the men at a nearby table, she smiled while watching the dancers. Blinking several times, in order to clear her blurring vision, she irrationally decided she wanted another one. Not normally one for bold moves she bravely decided to join him at the bar, thinking he might like the company.

Seeing Kalabernus was still sitting alone for the moment, she got up and stumbled toward him. Her head felt light and there was a faint buzzing sensation within her. The closer she came to him the more agitated she seemed to get. He exuded almost a dangerous quality about him and yet there was something about the way he looked at her that made her think he was anything but. Sareena couldn't seem to help herself, she wanted to be near him. It felt as though she were being drawn to him somehow.

"I'll have another fuzzy navel, please," Sareena called to the bartender above the noise. Her gaze shifted shyly to Kalabernus and she bumped his side with her hip while attempting to lean against the bar.

"You want... you want I cover it for you?" Kalabernus stammered, his mouth going dry at her close proximity. Her eyes appeared sleepy, giving them a sexy quality, he rather liked.

"And why might you do that?" Sareena smiled, accepting the wine cooler from the bartender. She twisted the top off and took a long drink.

"Seems a good exchange for your company, unless you're afraid. Most women are."

"I'm not afraid of you," Sareena replied quickly. "And you don't have to buy me a drink to gain my company." Her head drooped to one side and she gave him a flirtatious look, not realizing she was acting out of character. Usually, she was extra cautious with men she didn't know.

Choking on his beer Kalabernus coughed. Feeling a thrilling sensation as her hand pressed against his chest in concern, he covered hers with his own. Her soft skin felt good within his. They chatted for a while, garnering looks from several of the local regulars as well as Kahner near the pool table. After a while, Kalabernus noticed Sareena seemed very loose and drowsy in appearance, barely able to keep her eyes open.

"I could... I could give you a lift home if you like?" Kalabernus offered with a suggestive grin, not really expecting her to accept.

"Hhhhmmm, a ride home. Why not?" she giggled. Feeling dizzy and slightly disoriented she lost her balance and stumbled into him. "I think...I think I might need a bed anyway," Sareena stammered. Feeling his arms wrap around her for support, she moaned softly at the feel of him pressed up against her chest.

Startled by her response Kalabernus inquired, "You sure about that? You sure you're not afraid of me?"

"Oh, I've already danced with the devil. You're an angel in comparison."

"You might be surprised," he replied wryly while helping her to her feet. His gaze roamed the room, noticing the shadows flitting about, for once not paying any heed to him, which was odd.

Grabbing her jacket and purse for her from the back of her chair, he took her hand in his and guided her toward the front door. If he was quick, he might get her out the door before his brothers could waylay him. Women never expressed interest in him other than to look, and he didn't want to lose the chance of spending more time with her alone.

Watching the exchange with interest, the bartenders' brows rose as he witnessed the woman leave with Kalabernus. He'd never seen a woman express interest other than a casual glance, let alone to leave with him. Catching sight of Angela searching the room for her friend moments later he called out to her, gaining her attention.

"She left, Angela."

"Wait, what?" Angela responded, becoming alarmed.

Kalturek and Drayke sidled up to the bar for more beers.

"Your friend, she left with Kalabernus," Avery replied with a shrug. He gestured toward the door, then glanced with a smirk at the RavenCrofts while wiping down a few beer mugs. Both men peered back at him in surprise.

"Kalabernus left with a woman?" Drayke asked, mouth gaping in shock. Quickly regaining his composure, he chuckled and smirked knowingly.

"Not just any woman but that black haired bombshell you came in with Angie. Who is she anyway?" Kahner asked. Returning from the pool table he'd noticed his brother leaving and had been surprised he hadn't said anything.

Confused and appearing disturbed Angela grabbed her jacket, hastily putting it on. "That's impossible. Sareena would have never left with him willingly."

"Now just a minute…" Drayke became cross at the implication she was making.

"No, you don't understand," she snapped. She was visibly agitated. "Sareena had a stalker after her for nearly five years, and he messed with her head something fierce. It's why she moved here from Massachusetts to get away from him. Sareena would have never left with someone she didn't know. This is completely out of character for her," she declared, alarming the men present.

"Don't know what to tell you, but she did leave with him willingly," Avery said, wanting to make it clear that Kalabernus hadn't done anything wrong. "She did seem kind of loopy, though. Definitely wasn't afraid. Seemed odd considering." The bartender tried to be tactful. Everyone knew about Kalabernus's off-putting tendency.

Grabbing hastily for her purse Angela knocked over the wine cooler bottle on the table where she'd been sitting. Setting the bottle upright, she noticed part of a small round card peeking out from under the napkin it had been sitting on. Pulling the card out she turned it over and gasped, her hand trembling as she stared down at it. The four-inch circle had her friend's picture on it, and the face had been crossed out with a red X.

Shrieking in dismay Angela grabbed up the bottle on the table and shook it before the bartender. The bottle wasn't the same as what her friend had been drinking.

"Avery, where did this come from?"

"Angie, what's the matter?" Kalturek could see a dark hazy light surrounding her which was highly unusual. Normally when he'd look at Angela it was, at the very least, a pale white light.

"She's been drinking Fuzzy Navel's all night, not Strawberry Daiquiri's!" Angela shrieked, staring toward the door in dismay. "Kalturek you have to go after them and stop Kalabernus!" she insisted urgently.

Taking the round card from her hand, Kahner peered down at it uneasily. "Angela, what is this?" His gut clenched at the sight of a red X over the woman's face. He passed it on to Kalturek to see.

"It's the stalkers calling card!" Panicked tears swam in Angela's eyes.

Grabbing the bottle from her as the men exchanged worried looks Drayke sniffed at it and stared down at the card in Kalturek's hand.

"Would you say she seemed disoriented?" Drayke asked Avery suspiciously.

"Man, she fell into him," Avery said. "Almost looked like flirting but…"

"Are you thinking what I'm thinking?" Drayke asked his brother's darkly, alarmed by the possibility of what was running through his head and what it might mean.

"What I'm thinking, is that woman was likely drugged from the sounds of it." Kahner took the bottle from his brother and eyed it closely. He then waved it under his nose. "I'm betting probably ecstasy. There's no odor."

"And I'm thinking we need to find her now before Kalabernus accidentally does something potentially stupid with her." Internally Kalturek groaned. If the woman gave his brother even the slightest hint that she might be a willing participant in any carnal activity he knew his brother would be lost. It had been too long.

"He wouldn't take her back to the house and Dad has already re-rented his cabin. But honestly Angela, I don't see him doing that sort of thing anyway. If she's acting drunk, he's probably just trying to be a gentleman and give her a lift home. Where does she live?" Kahner asked thoughtfully, turning toward Angela.

Angela shook her head in distress, her chest heaving as she began to cry. "She just moved here, and we met at the bar. I don't know!"

Chapter 3

Uh, Oh.

That can't be good.

We have an extremely emotionally stunted man who is inexperienced where women are concerned and who hasn't had a date with one since sweet little Stacey Lynn died fourteen years before.

We also have a drop-dead gorgeous woman who thinks she's escaped the clutches of a stalker who, in fact, managed to chase her all the way from Dalton, Massachusetts in order to spike her drink with ecstasy.

Clearly, this is a recipe for disaster.

But the real question here is this. Was the stalker intending for Sareena to be taken home by someone else? Kalabernus, for example?

Somehow, I have the feeling that stalker of hers screwed up. What do you think? And what do you think this guy is going to do upon realizing that Kalabernus is making off with his woman?

I can't imagine anything good is going to come of any of this but you're sure to find out soon enough. Until then, what I should probably clarify for you, is that this poor woman, Sareena Davis, has been trying to gain freedom from her stalker for over five years now. After what happened to her old roommate back in Massachusetts about a month ago, fear propelled her to make some drastic decisions, and thereby changes, in her life. One of which was moving cross country to Loveland, Colorado from her life-long home with little to no warning to anyone.

You might be wondering, why Colorado?

That's answered easily enough.

You see, up to that point, Sareena's entire life had been on the East Coast. She was born there, raised there, and buried her sister then later her parents there. She even went to college there. But...

...One of her college friends was from Loveland, Colorado which is a fact only a handful of people knew. And Sareena had been smart enough to stay in touch with Angela Powers periodically over the years. So, when Sareena first thought to escape her stalker, she joked with Angela during one of her weekly phone conversations about pitching a tent in Angela's backyard. From there the idea bloomed and a plan was hatched. Problem was, as much as Sareena tried to keep everyone from suspecting her plan and where she was going, somehow the stalker got tipped off.

Boy, was he mad when he found out.

What do you think such a terrible, sick, and twisted individual does when they get mad?

Stir up 'trouble,' of course.

And we most definitely have some 'trouble' brewing.

Cause our stalker left the bar without Sareena Davis at his side as he'd originally planned after seeing her leave with Kalabernus. So naturally, this guy is mad as…

Well… I think you know where I'm going with that. You feel free to fill in the blank as you see fit because the author doesn't want me swearing in this here book of hers. Sheesh!

Anyway, as I was saying, the stalker is livid beyond reason. It doesn't help that he has a bunch of shadows messing with his head either. One thing is for sure, things are about to get messy because he already knows where Kalabernus is being directed to take her. What he doesn't fully understand yet, is who owns it.

Hhhmmm. Now, why would that matter?

Incidentally, I feel I should probably warn you that we're about to get into some inappropriate behavior here. And you'll likely find that this seems to become a running theme within the many stories of the RavenCroft family. Understand, I am by no means attempting to perpetuate bad behavior by sharing these series of events. What I am trying to do is point out that nowadays, people tend to create some challenging situations for each other to have to attempt to overcome. I think you'll find that most people have a questionable past in one form or another and that there are very few, if any, people out there without secrets whose life is completely without sin. Sorry folks, no better way of putting it than that.

The RavenCroft's are not bad people. What they are, however, is human, and therefore, often flawed in their thinking and actions. What soon becomes clear is that Kalabernus and even Sareena, for that matter, are particularly screwed up. In large part as the result of outside influences such as, I don't know, maybe a stalker and shadowy demonic creatures? I would imagine you'll start to understand better why this is, as the story progresses, so please be patient and wade past anything you might find a bit offensive. Because the actions of the individuals involved are more than just questionable. In fact, they're morally wrong. But in order to understand how and why they find themselves in so much 'trouble,' you need to have a bit of background. And some of it is likely going to be a little hard for some of you to swallow.

But then again, life is often a lot messier than what we'd like it to be. Wouldn't you agree?

- - -

Kalabernus promptly took off from Shenanigans in the general direction Sareena pointed him. By then she was acting giddy and playful, so it was a bit of a challenge for him to get her to tell him where he needed to go from there. After several minutes of prodding, he finally managed to learn the exact location and address of her home. He nearly skidded off the road in surprise when he discovered where she lived.

The woman he was driving home had apparently rented his cabin from his father by way of the rental agency. Kalabernus was pleased to be taking her home to where he still deemed as his home, even though he no longer actually lived there. The conversation on the drive there had been light but fun, leaving him marginally hopeful that he might be invited in for a cup of coffee. She seemed awfully nice and he couldn't help but be reminded of sweet Stacey Lynn. His heart tugged at the memory and his attention was drawn back to the road. He was determined to get her home safely.

After pulling in the drive and parking near the garage, he walked her to her door and assisted her into the house when she kept stumbling on her heeled boots. Asking him to stay for a bit, Sareena giggled while twirling about the living room, declaring happily that she was free. Chuckling at her behavior and unsure what to do next he'd simply watched her as she struggled out of her coat. Her jean jacket sleeve became stuck on her arm and she laughed, throwing her arm out toward him.

"It's stuck!" Sareena said, her eyes blinking slowly. "Help," she pleaded, giving the appearance of helplessness. She gazed up at him imploringly and he found he couldn't resist. Grinning, his fingers wrapped around her arm and he gently plied the jacket off the rest of the way.

Staggering away, still wearing her heeled boots, she headed toward the patio. Kalabernus chuckled. She'd admitted in the vehicle on the way home that she wasn't normally prone to wearing footwear with heels, but she'd seen the boots in the store window and had fallen in love. Clearly, she needed more practice walking in them.

"Where are you going?"

"Hot tub. Join me!" she called back.

Not fully aware of what she was doing and feeling very relaxed, she began to strip as she walked away. Humming softly, she threw her shirt aside and began unbuckling her belt buckle.

Kalabernus's jaw dropped. Was it possible this woman really wanted him to stay with her; as in sleep with her?

Hesitant, he followed her and stood in the patio doorway, astonished to see she'd completely undressed. Initially, he turned to leave, thinking he shouldn't be seeing her like this. His back to her, he pinched his eyes closed in frustration, the sight of her body imprinted upon his eyelids. Sweat beaded upon his brow as he turned back and caught the full view of her once again. She stood unabashedly in the hot tub, gazing out onto the lawn through the patio doors. He wiped at his forehead feverishly, having become uncomfortably warm at the sight of her. She was very pleasing to the eye. He supposed were he a better man that he should look away rather than drink his fill of her with his eyes. Kalabernus wrongfully rationalized his behavior away with the thought that if he were the sort to see and hear demons then he wasn't ever meant to be a good man at all.

His reaction to her bared state was immediate and he struggled to tame his inner turmoil. It had obviously been way too long since he'd been with a woman. But then, because most women were afraid of him, he'd only ever had one sexual experience in his lifetime. And that foray had ended horribly. So, he'd taken his father's words about intimacy and marriage to heart and decided it was best to abstain from such activity. Truthfully, he craved more of an emotional level of relationship than a purely physical one. But he was a man after all and her beauty was quite evident.

Watching her for a little while from a distance couldn't hurt anything, he thought, so he stood, leaning against the door jamb, appreciating the sight of her as she sat in the tub.

Kalabernus wasn't stupid. He sensed the woman might be a little tipsy and knew he had no business messing with her if she was. She clearly wasn't in her right mind now. If she were, she'd likely be running from him, screaming.

Eyes glazing over as he admired her beauty, Kalabernus suddenly realized her head was lolling back against the edge of the tub precariously. He straightened, sensing something was wrong as several shadows erupted unexpectedly from the corners of the patio. She seemed to be having difficulty keeping her eyes open. An alarm went off in his head when he saw her head sliding down into the water.

"She's not your concern!" he heard a dark spirit hissing as Kalabernus took off toward the hot tub. His sure-footed steps across the patio were swift and quiet. The cool night air drifting in through the open patio window began to clear the fantasies from his head. With each frantic step toward her, he could see her eyes growing heavier until finally they lost their battle and closed over those pretty gray eyes. Panic seized him as he watched the back of her head slide into the water.

"What's one more woman?" the shadow Zalman croaked next to his ear as he plunged into the water.

"Let her go, Kalabernus!" the dark spirit called Fallon spoke as it soared over his head and around him, as though attempting to bar him from the woman. Lifting her head up by her neck with his right hand, Kalabernus placed his left arm under her knees and lifted her up out of the water. Her weight in his arms surprised him slightly. She'd appeared lighter than what she was, not that it was an issue. He was a very strong man and could still easily carry her.

"Fat witch! Only one thing they're good for!" Zalman howled, cackling hoarsely. The shadows converged, floating eerily around him attempting to encase him in their essence.

"Enough!" Kalabernus shouted, growing tired of their incessant presence.

He stepped out of the tub and glanced down at the woman in his arms. Her face was flushed, and her body felt hot and wet to the touch. Kalabernus didn't even notice he was wet. He stood there for what seemed like an hour staring down at her soft wet body.

Boy, did she have curves.

Staring blatantly and openly upon her, he imagined what it might be like to be intimate with her. His breathing became ragged and he lost all train of thought. What was he doing with this naked woman in his arms?

He had to lay her down.

Check her pulse.

Make sure she was still alive. Her head had fallen into the water after all. But in the short span of time he thought this, her soft gray eyes flitted open.

Sareena gazed up at Kalabernus through foggy eyes. Even viewing him in her groggy state she could see he was the most mind-numbingly gorgeous man she'd ever known. Raising her free arm, she cupped his jaw tenderly in her hand and sighed against him.

"Leave her." This time, it was Veranke who spoke as he swirled in front of Kalabernus and took the shape of a faceless man. "There are other women more beautiful. Willing and ready to be…"

"I wonder what it is about her that is frightening you so." Kalabernus cut the foul creature off, mumbling loudly to himself. He chose instead to ignore the dark shape as he gazed upon her delicate features.

"Who are you talking to Kalabernus?" Sareena whispered softly, her thick voice sending a thrill down his spine. The movement of her lips drew his attention and his mind went numb.

"The shadows," he responded without thinking.

"Yes, sometimes the shadows talk to me, too," she said sadly, not fully aware of her state of undress. Her mind kept shifting in and out, as though in a half waking, half sleeping state.

Suddenly the shadows began swirling and whirling around the room, chattering incessantly as though frightened by something they'd seen. They pummeled around the patio as if they were being chased, stopping in the corners as though having been trapped there. Then without warning, they fled from the patio, soaring out into the moonlit sky. The behavior of the shadows did not faze Kalabernus, though he watched them closely till they disappeared. They were tricky blighters and had a tendency to make their presence known quite unexpectedly.

Thankful for the reprieve, however, brief it might be, he found he was now able to give the woman in front of him his full attention.

"Let's get you to bed." He spoke softly, his crystal-clear blue eyes mere slits as he adjusted her carefully in his arms to a more secure hold and carried her from the patio. He was unconcerned by the water dripping from them to the hardwood floor as he padded down the hallway. His hands trembled as he held her, wanting to do more than just carry her down the hall to her room - his old room. But he knew he couldn't do anything more then put her to bed, that he didn't dare go any further then plant an affectionate kiss on her forehead.

Nuzzling against his warmth Sareena sighed once again. "Yes, take me to bed Kalabernus."

Her words halted him at the bedroom doorway. Staring down at her, their eyes met and held for the longest time.

Was she fully lucid?

She appeared to be.

Kalabernus spoke low, his tone gravelly from repressed need and indecision. His conscience was chipping away at him. "Are...are you sure?" The excitement was building within him as a surge of blood rushed to his ears and to his head, clouding his better judgment.

"Hhhmm. Yes." Sareena felt sleepy. She was unaware she was answering an entirely different question, though in the back of her mind something was nagging at her.

Kalabernus left the doorway, carried her to the bed, and lay her upon it. He shifted away as though to leave, but she held him in place with the gentle touch of her hand, not wanting to be alone yet. In Kalabernus's mind, she appeared acquiescent of his presence, of his touch, and he wanted nothing more than to please her in that way if she was truly agreeable. Though he knew he shouldn't.

But was she agreeable?

No.

He shook his head violently, attempting to gain some semblance of control. What was wrong with him? No, no, no. He needed to cover her and leave, allowing her to sleep in peace.

Breathing heavily, he felt her lean in awkwardly toward him in the same moment he attempted to lean toward her to cover her with blankets. His left cheek brushed lightly against the soft skin of her jaw and his breath wafted near her ear. The sudden burst of heat at her presence so close to him sent his face flaming as though on fire. A tingling sensation ran the length of his spine causing his body to shake as hers trembled and a soft sound escaped her throat. He watched for any sign of reticence on her part, his gaze never wavering from her mesmerizing silvery eyes as his lips bore upon hers tentatively at first, then more intimately.

Chapter 4

I think that's where I'm going to have to cut in.

And yes, in case you're wondering both Kalabernus and Sareena are about to make a pretty bad choice as is implied, but we won't be going into those details here.

Yeah, I know. You're probably groaning, banging your head, and grumbling things like, "Come on, Vortigern! It's just getting to the good part. Why do you have to cut that out?"

Here's the thing. That danged author of this here story of 'trouble' and woe has insisted that this tale must be free of adult content, and therefore, inappropriate details of intimate exchanges are a big no, no.

I know, I know, what a prude, right? Believe you me, I argued on your behalf people. But the author was sure insistent. This here collection of mystery, thriller, suspense and romance books revolving around the RavenCroft family story must be free of what she deems as "smut." Kind of harsh, don't you think? I mean, really. What's wrong with a little titillating snippet of intimacy between the sheets, I say? But…the author sure seemed to think it particularly inappropriate under the circumstances, because as she so irritatingly points out, Sareena isn't really in the condition where she should be making such decisions, to begin with. And Kalabernus isn't thinking right now with his head but with other parts of his anatomy which will remain nameless.

Can you blame him, though? Any red-blooded male worth his salt would be struggling at her bedside were he in Kalabernus's shoes. Cause that Sareena Davis… Woohoo! She is a gorgeous lady, yes indeed!

I want to be really clear here, though. I'm not saying what's happening is right.

By no means.

Nope, nope.

That's not what I'm saying here. Even I would agree that this situation is simply wrong on so many levels. But let's consider the facts of what we know…that they don't know.

Factoid one, they both find each other attractive. (Okay, obviously they do know that.)

Factoid two, they both had a couple drinks. (All right, so they know that too.) But what you don't know and isn't shown here, is that Kalabernus does try to clarify from Sareena that she's not drunk before he takes things too far. To which she assures him she's not, thereby relieving him (he believes) of any potential wrong-doing other than sleeping with her out of wedlock.

Factoid three, neither of them are aware that she has been drugged as the result of her stalker. So, her amiable and complacent behavior is incorrectly construed as being flirtatious, inviting even, and therefore a consenting party.

Now before you get all huffy and stop reading because you're disgusted that someone would "take advantage" of someone like that, let me ask you something. How many times in your own life have you taken advantage of someone? And I don't necessarily mean in a situation like this. It could be that you ordered a more expensive meal and a bottle of wine rather than a glass when you found out your date had money. Or maybe you became "friends" with a co-worker to wheedle your way into their project to get in good with your boss.

Right now, you're probably thinking something like, "Now, Vortigern, you can't compare those things with what is happening here. It's not the same because no one is getting hurt in these instances."

Are you sure about that?

Or maybe you get that part but you're thinking this is an unrealistic scenario for a love story and that Kalabernus is a horrible human being.

Hhhmmm.

Does one bad choice make a person a horrible human being?

Or is it that good people can sometimes make bad choices?

And before you consider this an unrealistic situation, how many times in your own life have you known people who have made bad decisions but, in the end, things turned out all right?

Shoot, I can understand and even appreciate their situation. Should they be messing around like this at all? Well, that depends on your beliefs and how you were raised. In the case of the RavenCroft's, regardless of their lack of faith, Bastion and his late wife Inara did raise their children with some high moral standards, all things considered. After all, just because a person isn't religious, doesn't mean they're immoral. A person can be raised within an environment and with certain belief systems and yet still make poor choices in the heat of the moment. Wouldn't you say? After all, we are human. And as humans, we make many, many bad choices over time.

But not me.

Because as I've said before, I'm perfect. No bad choices here. But you already know that.

Oh, there she goes again. The author is rolling her eyes at me. Huh. She's sure been doing that a lot lately.

Anyway, some of you are probably thinking that Kalabernus is a clod of the worst kind, am I right? Because as far as you're concerned, regardless of whether he's aware of the drug or not, he's taking advantage of a woman who appears to be, maybe, a bit tipsy. Now, I'll give you, there may be something to that. And I'm not going to sit here and attempt to justify his actions. But the author did seem to think that I would be remiss in my duties as narrator if I didn't point out that this man has been tortured by shadows all his life. That's forty years of torment people. What would your response be if you were him?

Before we're so quick to judge others, we need to be able to understand them and what they've lived through.

Regardless of being raised in a house with high moral standards, one could argue that the incessant badgering of the shadowy demonic creatures has worn down the man's resistance in addition to his moral compass. More so, at least, than most. A person can know that something is wrong and yet not have a full grasp or understanding of the ramifications of what's happening now. I, Vortigern Black, personally feel that it's really a wonder the man didn't wind up growing up to become a sociopath or murderer rather than a painter of fine art. In the end, though, it's how an individual responds or acts after they've made a bad choice that shows the true nature of their character. But don't take my word for it...

- - -

Kalabernus awoke to the sound of someone banging on the front door. Somewhat disoriented initially, it took a minute for him to realize he was not in his bed at the RavenCroft ranch, but for some reason lying in a bed in his cabin.

The initial surprise at finding he was holding a woman in his arms wore off quickly as the memory of being intimate with Sareena came back to him instantly. He would have laid still next to her, trying to decide the best way to unravel from her without waking her, but the incessant pounding wouldn't stop.

Hoping he could get to the door before she fully awoke from the noise, he quickly threw on his jeans, barely managing to zip them before reaching the front door. Flinging the door wide Kalabernus found himself face to face with his brother Kalturek.

"What are you doing here?" Kalabernus growled, blinking in the bright lights of the Sheriff's cruiser parked in the drive.

Taking in the sight of Kalabernus's bare chest and partially zipped jeans Kalturek groaned. Fisting his hand against his forehead as he leaned against the door jamb he cringed at the sound of car doors opening and closing behind him. He sensed movement coming up the walk.

"Please tell me you didn't sleep with Sareena Davis," Kalturek practically begged. He tried to keep his voice down so those coming up the walk couldn't hear.

Becoming indignant Kalabernus scowled. "What business is it of yours anyway if I did?"

Head drooping, Kalturek groaned, having gotten his answer and not liking it a bit. "Because she's been drugged," he replied urgently.

"Is she there? Is she okay?" Angela called, hurrying past Kahner and Drayke. Stopping abruptly at the sight of Kalabernus's shocked gaze staring back at his brother, she lifted a hand to her lips and gasped. Eyes widening in dismay at the sight of him barefoot and clad only in jeans, she understood instantly what had happened.

"Angela, stay back. Kalturek will handle this." Drayke insisted, aggravated that she'd forced them to bring her along. It would have been better if Angela hadn't been present.

"What do you mean she's been drugged?" Kalabernus inquired, stunned.

"We think someone spiked her drink with ecstasy at the bar," Kahner supplied, peering at his brother's startled gaze with sympathy.

Eyes narrowing, Kalabernus's jaw clenched angrily. "Oh, right. Because that would be the only way a woman like that would ever want to be with me. Is that right? Is that what we're saying here?" Shoving away from the door frame he spun away walking back into the living room. They followed him inside.

"Just listen Kalabernus…"

"Where is she?" Angela demanded, her gaze darting about the room.

"I buried her out back," Kalabernus said snidely.

"That's not funny!" Angela shouted, instantly becoming hysterical.

"Angie?" A weak voice called from down the hallway.

Kalabernus turned in time to see Sareena wobbling into view. She was completely naked. Horrified he leaped over the couch and rushed across the room, grabbing the knitted blanket from the chair as he ran. Covering her with the blanket so she couldn't be seen, he reached around and caught her before she began to slip to the floor.

"Whoa, there, Honey. I got you," Kalabernus said gently next to her. Gazing down into her confused and disoriented expression an uneasiness filled the pit of his stomach. Could he really have just had sex with a woman who'd been drugged? Was that why she'd been so complacent? So unafraid and willing?

"You got me?" Sareena asked peering up at the man holding her in a daze. "Who's you?" she asked, struggling to keep her eyes open.

"Who's me? Wait. Wait, wait…you mean you don't remember?" Kalabernus stammered, appearing both horrified and hurt. He searched her face. Pleading internally for her to remember. It couldn't possibly have been just one-sided.

Kalturek winced, baring his teeth as he exchanged awkward pained looks with his brothers. He noted Angela was watching Kalabernus shrewdly, her hawk-like gaze narrowing on him as her expression became pinched and angry.

Head bobbing dreamily, Sareena peered over at the people in the living room, unclear as to what was going on and who they were. Recognizing Angela, she latched onto her. Though sensing she somehow knew the man next to her, she was unable to place him for some reason.

"He's beautiful Angela. Who is he?"

"Uh, oh." Drayke supplied awkwardly.

"No!" Pulling away from her, Kalabernus leaned Sareena up against the wall. He wanted to make sure she didn't fall but was more than a little upset she couldn't remember him. Particularly after what had happened between them.

"Kalabernus, man. She was drugged," Kahner interjected, trying to assuage the guilt he could already see emerging in his brother's expression to no avail.

"By who?" Kalabernus raged. His eyes were fierce, fixing them with a dark stare.

Kalturek produced the card they'd found on the table. "It would appear she has a stalker. He's been after her for nearly…"

"Five years!" Angela shouted. "What's the matter with you Kalabernus? She was probably what? Stumbling about and slurring words, like a drunk maybe? How could you take advantage of her like that?"

Though alarmed to learn of the stalker, Kalabernus became defensive at Angela's accusation. Whirling toward the front door his gaze shifted toward Sareena than back at Angela and his brothers.

"I…take advantage? No! But she wanted… She said she… I swear I didn't…!"

Gasping audibly at the sight of her stalker's calling card in Kalturek's hand Sareena stumbled away down the hallway. She was slowly starting to comprehend at least part of what was happening. Her stalker was back, and he'd done something to her - again.

"Angela? Where…where did that come from?" Sareena exclaimed with fright, pointing toward Kalturek with a shaking finger.

"It was on our table and…"

"It was near *you?*" Sareena shrieked in distress. "Angela are you saying he was near *you?*" she cried fearfully. Her terrified eyes bore into her friend, desperately wanting what was happening not to be real.

"Yes, Honey. I'm so sorry. And we think…we think he spiked your drink with ecstasy," Angela explained uneasily.

Peering over at the very large and beautiful man standing guiltily in the entryway, understanding finally dawned in Sareena's beautiful gray eyes. Frightened tears streamed down her cheeks. She stared at her friend, the woman she'd known since her college days and all she could see was the lifeless face of her roommate, Kami.

"You have to go," Sareena demanded. Her voice was hollow, the sheer terror within alarming even Kalabernus. "*Now!*" she shouted at Angela.

Flinching, Angela stared back at her, not fully understanding why her friend was demanding that she leave. "No, Sareena you don't understand..." she began with a nervous smile. Grabbing the card from Kalturek she attempted to move toward Sareena.

"No! *You* don't understand!" Sareena screamed in a blind panic. "It can't happen again! I won't let it happen again! Get out, Angela, *get out!*"

"Sareena, Honey, I know you've been hurt." Angela cast an accusatory glance Kalabernus's way. "I'm your friend. I just want to help."

"No! No, you're not my friend," Sareena said sharply, charging toward her, all the while holding the blanket tightly in place. "Do you understand me Angela Powers? You're not my friend. You can never be my friend," she declared, enunciating each word clearly. "I don't ever want to see you again. Do you understand me? Get out of my house!" Sareena continued to yell as she wobbled around the room her gaze shifting wildly from one wall to the next. "Do you hear me? Do you hear me, you miserable cur? She's not my friend. She's never been my friend and she'll never be my friend. None of you can ever be my friend. Get out. *Get out!* Get out of my house!" Sareena screamed. A mixture of resentment, anger, and terror fueled her voice as she shook violently, pointing all the while toward the front door.

Hysterical tears streamed down Angela's cheeks as she fled the house into the yard, sobbing and clearly hurt.

Urging his brothers out of the cabin, Kalturek attempted to approach Sareena. Concerned by the woman's reaction to Angela, his gaze shifted uneasily toward Kalabernus who simply stood in the entryway, staring back at her, a look of shock on his face.

"Ms. Davis. There's still the matter of what happened here tonight."

"No. No, there isn't." Sareena spoke in a deathly quiet voice. Shaking her head, she began to sob as she peered over at Kalabernus, a pained look on her face as she spoke into her hands. "Nothing happened worth mentioning," she said quietly, her words clipped and void of emotion. But the tears wetting her cheeks and the fear in her eyes as she looked up at Kalturek said otherwise.

Kalabernus disappeared swiftly through the front door, not bothering to go back for his shirt and shoes. Staggering down the front steps, Kalturek on his heels, Kalabernus heard the door shut loudly behind them. The click of the lock and deadbolt signified an end to any further discussion.

Not paying attention to where he was going, Kalabernus bumped into Angela while attempting to sprint down the walkway barefooted.

"Why you always gotta be present when I'm in pain?" Kalabernus yelled at her angrily.

Flinching, Angela cowered initially, still attempting to recover from her longtime friend screaming at her and kicking her out of her home. Becoming angry at her cowardice and his belligerence Angela quickly recovered, pulling herself up to her full five-foot-five-inch height.

"Why you always gotta be present when I lose a friend?" she snapped back, instantly regretting her words. The look on Kalabernus's face was of a man who had just been slapped. "I'm sorry!" Angela cried suddenly, realizing how cruel she'd been.

Kalabernus pushed past her, hands balling into fists at his sides. Clearly hurt and trying to pretend he wasn't, he sauntered down the drive away from them.

"Wait, Kalabernus!" Kalturek glared back at Angela.

"Was that really necessary?" Kahner growled, shooting her a dirty look.

"I lost someone that night too, you know?" Angela yelled, becoming angry once again. They all acted like Kalabernus was the only one affected by Stacey's death. "And I know you all know something you're not telling me. So, don't act like you're all innocent. Especially you Kalabernus."

"I never said I was innocent!" Kalabernus roared. Turning abruptly on his heels, he charged back toward her. "Stacey died because of me fourteen years ago just as sure as Sareena was violated by me here tonight," he yelled, waving his arm toward the house. "You think I don't know I'm a monster? You think I don't know I'm feared by both women and men just for being in the same room?" The pain reflecting in his brilliant pale blue eyes was excruciatingly heart wrenching to witness.

Huddled near the window inside the cabin, Sareena could see the haunted look in Kalabernus's eyes and knew she had caused it. She was the reason he was in pain. She was the reason everyone around her ever experienced pain. Her nightmare hadn't really gone away after all. She couldn't run from it. Shoot, she couldn't even move half a dozen states away from it.

Sobbing uncontrollably, Sareena watched the giant of a man flee toward his vehicle. She'd seen and overheard it all. Trembling uncontrollably, she crawled toward the stand near the chair clutching at the blanket wrapped around her. With shaky fingers, Sareena reached into the small jewelry box resting near the lamp. Pulling a small item from inside she clasped it tightly within the palm of her hand.

She'd had it since she was a little girl. Whenever she was most afraid Sareena would hold tightly to it and whisper a fervent prayer. She didn't know if anyone was listening or if God was even real. But what she did know of a certainty was that if she ever lost it she would lose her grip on reality. So, she held tightly to it with all her might and whispered her fervent prayer till sleep finally overtook her. The shadows swirled angrily about her as she slept, eager to put their devilish plans into action.

Chapter 5

Strolling into the Sheriff's department the next morning, Bastion RavenCroft paused in the entrance. He scowled when he observed his three sons: Kalturek, Kahner, and Drayke conversing urgently amongst themselves through the two-way glass window of the Sheriff's office. Snatching up a magazine on the light stand next to him he rolled it in his hands.

Ignoring the deputy's attempts to halt him at the receiving desk, he banged through the swinging door which separated the entryway from the deputy's cubicles and desks. Walking with purpose toward Kalturek's office Bastion's eyes narrowed to slits. He could see Drayke speaking with animation over the file he held in his hand, then unceremoniously dumping it on Kalturek's desk. Slapping his son's office door open with the palm of his right hand, Bastion glared at the three men within, equally disgusted with them all.

"Sareena Davis isn't even her real name," Kalturek was saying as Bastion entered loudly, gaining their attention.

Bastion grunted. "Of course, it isn't," he said in a matter-of-fact fashion while rounding Kalturek's desk.

"That's identity deception." Drayke's lips thinned as he pointed toward the file in Kalturek's hands.

"And forgery if she's used the social to obtain work." Kalturek agreed grimly.

"Right, because she would have signed an I-9 form upon filling out employment papers," Kahner said, snapping his fingers toward Drayke.

"We can get a copy of the original on Monday from her employer," Drayke supplied.

Tightening his grip on the rolled magazine Bastion whacked at Kalturek's head unexpectedly. Erupting from his chair irately, Kalturek flung his arms out toward his father after rubbing the side of his head.

"What was that for?" he hollered angrily. His gaze shifted toward the two-way window which allowed him to look out toward the cubicles in the outer office. He hoped none of his deputies had seen that. It would have been highly humiliating considering he was forty years old and a county Sheriff.

Bastion shook the rolled magazine before him, pointing it towards Kalturek, then his brothers.

"That... is for not calling me sooner!" Bastion growled darkly, his gaze shifting between his sons. "And as for Ms Davis's subterfuge, what do you expect? She was being stalked by someone and was trying to get away from them, I'd wager. Besides all of this is inconsequential in the light of the fact Kalabernus had sex with her while she was drugged!" Bastion vented in disgust, rounding on his sons.

"Yeah, but Dad. He didn't know that, and we can use this to protect Kalabernus..." Drayke began, only to be cut off with a swift smack on the head from his brother Kahner. "Hey!" he exclaimed irately.

"Geez, Drayke. You're the district's prosecuting attorney now, not a defense lawyer. Don't be thinking like some thug. And besides, Dad's right," Kahner said crossly, fully understanding what his father was getting at. "We'd be going after the victim rather than the person we need to be."

"The stalker," Kalturek said grimly in agreement. Pulling the file towards him, he set down in his desk chair. Opening it again he sifted through the papers, lifting each one out individually and scanning them quickly.

"That's right. Now, what is her name really?" Bastion inquired. "Do we know at least that yet?"

"Angela wasn't terribly forthcoming when I confronted her this morning about the deceased status of the background check on Sareena Davis," Kalturek explained.

"Small wonder," Drayke said, rolling his eyes. He dropped lazily down into the chair in front of Kalturek's desk, propping his dress shoes up on it.

Shooting his brother a dirty look, Kalturek grabbed the magazine and flung it at his brother's feet. Drayke chuckled and grinned, crossing one leg over another as he leaned back, uncaring that he was aggravating his brother. Leaping hastily from his chair Kalturek grabbed the file folder and began whacking at his brother's feet vigorously.

Watching the exchange from a mere few feet away, Kahner began laughing, his eyes twinkling with mirth.

"Would you two knock it off? I swear it's like the three of you never grew up," Bastion hollered.

"You're only as old as you feel, Dad." Kahner laughed, watching the scene before him. He had missed his brother's antics and his father's ensuing wrath.

"Then I guess that makes me about two hundred years old then," Bastion shouted. "How did you become Sheriff anyway?" he asked crossly, directing his gaze toward Kalturek.

"I was elected as you well know. I happen to have a bright smile and winning good looks. You know that." Kalturek responded with a grin towards his brothers. His dad had always said he wouldn't amount to anything and had bet him he'd likely become a school janitor, cleaning toilets before he'd ever become Sheriff of Loveland County. Thinking to be funny and to spite him, Kalturek had proved him wrong and managed to get himself elected. He'd never forget the day they'd announced the election results. His dad had insisted on a recount of the ballots.

"*Enough!*" Bastion thundered over their laughter and smirking. "I think we have a pretty serious matter here, don't you? It deserves a little consideration."

"Right. No, you're right, Dad. Sorry," Kalturek said quickly, having been properly chastised.

Regaining his composure, he continued. "I did a little investigating and learned Ms. Davis has a sister by the name of Ariana. I suspect Sareena switched identities."

"Oh, that's pretty," Drayke breathed, mumbling under his breath. "Pretty name for a pretty lady.

Ignoring his brother Kalturek continued. "Now, Ms. Ariana Davis is alive and well and last known to have lived in Dalton, Massachusetts where she has numerous complaints about having been stalked by a rather relentless individual. It seems Sareena Davis, on the other hand, actually died at age sixteen from an auto accident."

Bastion grunted. The air within the room seemed to shift then freeze in place. "That's not true. It wasn't an accident," he said suddenly, "but continue."

The three men peered toward their father curiously. His unexpected bits of insight, on things he had no way of knowing of, were often disquieting to hear, but they believed him, nonetheless. Far too often Bastion was right.

"So, Ariana takes up the name of her deceased sister in the hopes of disappearing," Kahner spoke, "and leaving her stalker behind."

"It was a good thought. Could have worked too," Drayke observed with a heavy sigh.

"Not likely in this case," Kalturek disagreed.

"Why?" Drayke asked, head turning toward his brother curiously.

Lifting a page from the file he laid it out on his desk for all to see. "That's Kami Russell, her former roommate," Kalturek explained. "It would seem

Ariana came home to find her stabbed to death on the floor of their living room apartment. They had apparently argued the night before about whether Kami should move out in the interest of safety after receiving a threat against her, but Ariana had been unable to convince her friend otherwise. The stalker left this behind at the scene." Pulling out another page, he laid it next to the image. "The note left with her body said, 'Now you no longer have to worry.'"

Picking it up Kahner pulled the card left on the table the night before from his brother's desk and compared it to the one photocopied on the paper. Wincing, his gaze shifted to his father as he passed the card and paper over to him to view.

"It would seem our stalker is no longer having warm fuzzy feelings toward our Ms. Davis." The disquiet in Bastion's tone was obvious. His gaze roamed from one image to the next. The card left at the scene of Kami Russell's death was an image of Sareena, or more accurately Ariana Davis, encircled by a red heart shape. But the new card left last night had her X'd out, implying a more dangerous game was being played now.

"Do you think it changed maybe because she tried disappearing on him?" Drayke asked, having caught sight of the image on the paper.

"Anything is possible when dealing with nut jobs. The fact is, according to what I've read so far on her file, this all started innocently enough about five years ago," Kalturek replied.

"That's when she thinks it started anyway," Bastion offered. He gazed through the window outside Kalturek's office into the parking lot next door. His thoughts were jumbled and distracted and the image before him was hazy. The dreamlike vision of a small red crumpled car came into view then just as swiftly disappeared.

"Regardless, of whether it was sooner or not, her first inkling of anything was a note left on her vehicle outside of her work over five years ago. Her statements seem to suggest she thought it simply an admirer and responded as such, believing she suspected who it was. After several weeks of notes back and forth, left via her car windshield, she approached the individual only to learn he hadn't been pursuing her. That's when the notes started getting a little scarier. More possessive."

Bastion turned back toward his son. "Possessive how?"

"'Don't go to the movie with Derrick. You deserve better,'" Kalturek read aloud. Lifting a stack of papers, he continued to read more missives that had been left for her. "'I told you not to go. Don't worry I'll make sure he never asks again.' This one here says, 'Kami's such a whore, don't let her move in.' Another one later says, 'why won't you listen to me? You shouldn't have let her move in. Whatever happens now is on you.'" Kalturek continued to read, the messages becoming more and more disturbing in nature. "'I love you, Ariana, I'll never let you go. Only death shall part us.'"

"Was that the last one before this Kami Russell was killed?" Kalabernus inquired, startling everyone. His massive frame seemed to fill the room upon entering. He'd clearly been listening in for a while and no one present had been the wiser.

"How is it you manage to do that?" Kahner asked, thoroughly perplexed. Kalabernus was the only one, at times, that he had trouble sensing, or even reading for that matter.

"Don't know, don't care. Now, was that the last one before this Kami Russell was murdered?" Kalabernus demanded urgently.

"It would appear so," Kalturek said quietly, eyeing his brother cautiously. "Why do you ask?"

"Is Angela still dating Heaton, or are they, as I suspect, on the outs again?" Kalabernus inquired, not answering his brother. Their gazes locked and instantly Kalturek knew what he was thinking.

"You're thinking that's why Ariana responded to Angela the way she did last night, aren't you?" Kahner asked, having read his mind.

"Shoot, I got that without having to read his mind," Kalturek said wryly. "Drayke?"

Startled Drayke responded. "What?"

"Well, what do you know?"

"Know what?"

"Angela and Heaten, you git! What do you think I'm asking about?" Kalturek demanded.

"For the love! Just because everyone talks around me, doesn't mean..."

"Drayke," Bastion said with a warning tone, not caring whether he was embarrassed or not to be privy to the town's gossip pool as the result of his gift to glean the truth from people.

Huffing indignantly Drayke scowled. "Fine! Angela kicked him to the curb last Friday because he was apparently giving Marcy Lou eyes during the Kid's dunk-a-thon at the park."

"Marcy Lou?" Kahner asked, head jerking his direction. Lifting his hands into a circular motion in front of his chest he continued. "Isn't she the one with the really nice big…"

"Give it a rest," Bastion hollered, becoming cross.

"You need to get Heaton and Angela in here." Kalabernus insisted urgently, gazing towards his brother sitting behind his desk. "She needs protection, Kalturek, and he's the best she could possibly get considering he has a black belt."

"Oh, no. I am the Sheriff of Loveland County, not the county matchmaker," Kalturek responded firmly.

Growling Kalabernus yanked the picture of Kami Russell from the desk and shoved it in front of his brother's face. "Picture this as Angela Powers. We've known her since kindergarten, Kalturek! Trust me, you don't want that image in your head anymore then I want Stacey Lynn's lifeless face in mine." Shoving violently at the papers on the desk, he then stalked toward the door.

Calling after his son, Bastion saw him pause at the doorway. "Son, you need to talk to this woman, Ariana."

Kalabernus looked back at his father, his haunted eyes were filled with pain and regret. "No, I really don't." With a slight shake of his head, he walked away. His vast solid frame could be seen lumbering toward the entryway through the two-way window in the office.

Lifting his phone from the receiver Kalturek cleared his throat then spoke. "Mark. Do me a favor and get Heaton Jones and Angela Powers in here."

"You want I bring them in together?" Mark responded on the other end, sounding almost anxious. All the deputies were fully aware of the individual's explosive relationship.

"No. Send a car to pick up Angela. Have Heaton come in on his own." Hanging up Kalturek shoved back in his chair in aggravation. "Had I known matchmaking was a part of Sheriff's work I'd have never run for Sheriff," he declared, tossing the pencil he'd been twiddling in his hand at his desk.

"It serves you right for spiting me and becoming Sheriff," Bastion said forcefully, unable to completely mask the glimmer in his eye as he spoke. He headed for the door.

"Where do you think you're going?" Kalturek cringed instantly when his father stopped and turned toward him. His expression was blank, completely void of emotion. Kalturek hated it when he'd get that way. It made him impossible to read.

"I have to go. There are things to do and people to see."

"People to see? We've got a mess here."

"No, you have a stalker to catch Sheriff RavenCroft," Bastion reminded, pointing at his son.

"He, or she, is your problem as well as the safety of Angela. The situation between Ariana and Kalabernus is between them and me."

"Wait, why you?" Kahner inquired, appearing confused. "What happened, occurred between them after all, and she is renting the cabin from him."

"The deed was never put in his name," Bastion supplied with a decisive shake of his head. He appeared agitated. "I never got around to it." Shifting his weight to one foot he kicked the door with the toe of his boot. "As the owner of said property, it falls to me to see to her safety. Being as I am aware that harm may have befallen my tenant while residing within her home, I will be speaking with her shortly. As should you be attempting to contact her and bring her in as well, I would imagine."

Bastion's gaze shifted to Drayke and Kahner as he moved toward the door. They were both attempting the appearance of nonchalance. Instead, they looked like a couple of idiots awaiting the impending ruckus between Angela and Heaton. He rolled his eyes in disgust. "For heaven sake. Drayke, go back to work, and Kahner, go home to your pregnant wife and kids. Thirty-eight and forty years old respectively and you all still act like children."

Chapter 6

Vortigern Black here again.

I know, I know. You're probably getting tired of hearing from me, eh?

No worries. I'm not going to take you out of this story any more than necessary because I know it's starting to get really good cause our Ms. Sareena Davis turned out not to be who we thought she was. It seems her name is Ariana Davis and that she took up her sister's name to get away from her stalker. Technically speaking what she did was illegal but honestly, can you blame her? The police department back in Massachusetts wasn't having any luck in figuring out who her stalker was, and Ariana's roommate had been murdered by him. Up to that point, the stalker had been more of a nuisance than a real threat. But then, for some reason, his tactics had escalated, and no one seemed to know why.

Eventually, Ariana will have a bit of a mess to clean up because of assuming her deceased sister's identity.

Bank accounts and even her lease was all created in Sareena's name. Only her trusted long-distance employer was aware of her deception, or so she'd thought.

Fortunately, Kalabernus showed up at his brother's office when he did because he pointed out a potential danger to their friend Angela that the others hadn't picked up on yet. Oh, they would have eventually figured it out but Kalabernus's protective instincts were on high alert after what had happened between him and Ariana the night before. You could say he was extra vigilant now for it occurred to him that the stalker hadn't intended for Ariana to get a ride home with him. That likely meant he may well have angered a murderer.

Angela was not only a college friend of Ariana's but a long-time friend of the RavenCroft family. Learning that Ariana's former roommate had been killed simply because of moving in with her, Kalabernus was determined to make sure Angela's safety was seen to. He knew he couldn't keep track of both women, and he wanted to try and protect Ariana from this stalker if it was at all within his power. He felt it was the least he could do under the circumstances and besides, he was looking for a little payback himself.

- - -

There was a phone ringing. Yet the lethargy Ariana was feeling as she slowly came to a waking state prevented her from investigating its source. Her eyes felt heavy, her throat dry and pasty.

The phone stopped ringing.

Ariana swiftly slipped back into a restless sleep.

What seemed like mere moments later, but was, in fact, an hour, Ariana woke with a start. The phone was ringing again, only this time her head didn't feel quite so foggy. Though it throbbed with each ring.

She pushed up from the living room floor where she lay, only for the afghan to slip down and tangle around her legs. Naked, she stumbled her way towards the incessant ringing. Locating the phone hanging on the wall between the bedroom and the kitchen Ariana grabbed it up without thinking, desperate to get the incessant ringing to stop. Summoning every ounce of energy she had Ariana managed a weak and groggy greeting as she attempted to regain her senses.

"Hello? Hello, Ms. Davis? This is Sheriff Kalturek RavenCroft of the Loveland Sheriff's Department. May I have a moment of your time?" he asked, sounding both awkward as well as a bit concerned.

Clearing her throat Sareena managed a thick sounding "No," then hung up.

The phone rang again before she could move down the hall. Not thinking straight, she answered it again.

"Sheriff RavenCroft here. I really need to speak with you Ms. Davis, about last night."

"There's nothing to talk about."

She hung up again.

Moments later the phone rang again, its incessant piercing sound jangling her nerves every time it resonated throughout the cabin. This time, she didn't bother picking it up.

- - -

Bastion stood on the doorstep of his son's cabin, observing the woman before him who had seconds before grudgingly opened her door to him. He noted she appeared to have just come from a shower. Her lustrous black hair hung in damp messy waves down her back and her face was free of makeup, not that she needed it.

"Ms. Davis, my name is Bastion RavenCroft. Might I have a moment of your time?"

"I'm sorry. What did you say your name was again?" Ariana inquired. Her hand reached up to shield her eyes from the bright piercing sunlight streaming through the doorway. The very large good-looking man before her was a bit intimidating both in size and stature even after having removed his black Stetson from his head the moment she'd opened her door. His short hair, salt and pepper in color, made him appear in his fifties. Sporting a long black duster and cowboy boots he appeared to have just stepped out of a western movie, or at the very least, off of a ranch.

"Bastion RavenCroft, at your service," he replied cordially, bowing slightly at the waist.

"RavenCroft," Ariana mumbled suspiciously, instantly on her guard. "You're related to the Sheriff and…"

"Kalabernus. Yes, ma'am, I am. I'm their father."

Ariana inhaled sharply. She stared at him, her face flushing with embarrassment. Recovering quickly her temper flared.

"I suppose he sent you here to deal with me?" Ariana asked, sounding more than a little peeved.

"No, actually. Kalabernus has no clue. And when he finds out I came to see you I'm likely not going to hear from him for the next year or so." Bastion spoke frankly. "That particular son of mine has a rather unforgiving nature, unfortunately."

"I see," she said quietly. Her expression became troubled. "So, I don't suppose he'll likely be accepting an apology from me anytime soon then, will he?"

Twin creases spread along Bastion's forehead as his brow rose in surprise. "Now what, Ms. Davis, would you possibly need to apologize to my son for?"

"It seems he was an unwitting victim of backlash from my stalker. He's been after me for five years now, and that's his way, you see. He hurts people around me for fun." Ariana's hand clamped around the door handle uneasily as she fidgeted before him. The way he was staring was making her nervous. "People I love are forever suffering from the repercussions of his wrath."

"Why do I get the feeling they're not the only ones?" Bastion said evenly, giving the woman a calculated look. He could see why his son might have had difficulty controlling himself with her. She was very beautiful indeed. Imagining that was likely the reason she'd drawn the attention of her stalker in the first place, he pursed his lips. Feeling almost a pulsing sensation around them, as though the air had been shifted in some way then abruptly returned to its normal state, Bastion came to a revelation which confirmed his suspicions. Her stalker had been following her a lot longer than she likely realized. Normally, his ability to see visions of past, present and future events wasn't a problem, but it was most bothersome when it happened while in the presence of someone other than family.

"Ms. Davis, do you intend to stay here?" Bastion inquired, nodding his head toward the cabin while trying to shake off the images.

"I...well, I signed a lease. Why wouldn't I?"

Bastion frowned, his brow furrowing further as he stood before her in her doorway, deep in thought. "Considering the nature of your situation, I wonder if moving closer to town might not be more prudent?"

"What do you mean?"

"This cabin is pretty far removed from town. Loveland county Sheriffs are known for their speed but even they have their limits. Chances are they might not make it in time should you find yourself in real trouble."

"I appreciate your concern Mr. RavenCroft, but even if I wanted to move, I've signed a lease for a year. And no offense, but I'm not sure any of this is really your concern," Ariana replied, his observation making her anxious.

"That's where you'd be mistaken. Aside from the fact you're a single woman in trouble, you also happen to be renting a cabin on my property which makes you my tenant. I'd just as soon not have any further incident occur on my land. Particularly when my hope is that one day my son might actually be able to live here again."

Ariana was stunned. Mouth agape she peered up at the RavenCroft patriarch in dismay. Tilting her head, a random thought popped into her mind as she stared at the same crystal-clear blue eyes she'd seen in Kalabernus and his other sons the night before.

"How old are you?" she asked, oblivious to the semi-impolite line of questioning. Her suspicious nature had returned giving her cause to question whether the man was truly who he said he was. There were familial similarities, but he appeared way too young to be their father.

Bastion smiled easily, the slight crow's feet near his eyes becoming momentarily more pronounced, which helped signify his aging state.

"I turn sixty in March if you must know."

"Bull crap." The words flew out of Ariana's mouth before she could stop them. Covering her mouth, her eyes widened in alarm for having spoken so rudely. "Oh, I'm so sorry!" She hadn't meant to be disrespectful.

Bastion laughed, amused by her genuine personality and unintentional, but much appreciated, compliment.

"You flatter me."

Managing to recover from her humiliation she cleared her throat and finally asked. "Mr. RavenCroft am I to understand that you're my landlord?"

"Yes, ma'am."

"And one of your sons used to live here?"

"You have good ears."

"Wait, Mr. RavenCroft…"

"Bastion, please. No need to stand on ceremony," he said waving his hand in the air dismissively.

"Bastion then. Which son are you referring to?"

"Why, Kalabernus of course."

"But of course!" Ariana exclaimed in further dismay, wondering how she could have such rotten luck. Shoving her fist in her mouth she bit at her knuckles as she attempted to think through her dilemma. "When you said, 'any further incident,' am I to understand you're fully aware of what transpired last night?" she inquired, somewhat horrified by the notion.

Sensing he needed to tread carefully, Bastion took an extra moment before responding. "I do understand the awkwardness of this situation for you. Rest assured, Kalabernus has been quite thin-lipped over the matter. That being said, I have been made aware of what may have occurred here last night by other parties and seek merely for answers to a few simple questions."

"Which are?" Ariana inquired, as anxiety flooded within her anew.

"First and foremost, are you okay? Please tell me, did my son hurt you?" Bastion asked urgently. "He is a very big man, as you well know, and I would hate to think any further harm might have come to you over this situation this stalker of yours created." He gazed at her intently, concern evident in his expression and tone.

Surprised by the initial query Ariana did a double take. Her response immediate, but quiet. "I am as well as I can be expected, but no. No, he didn't hurt me, that I recall." It was becoming quite clear to Ariana that Bastion RavenCroft was simply attempting to ascertain whether she'd been harmed.

"And do you still feel safe here? I would happily allow you out of your lease, should you desire to move closer to the town where you could gain quicker assistance if it became necessary. Please understand, I'm by no means kicking you out, just worried for your safety out here. If this stalker of yours can reach across states and into public bars to get to you, then he most certainly could reach you here."

Leaning against the door frame for support Ariana gazed around at her surroundings. There was a chill in the air which led her to believe the temperatures would be dropping soon. More of the golden and burgundy leaves would soon litter the lawn and she'd so looked forward to raking them up just to fling herself into them. She'd chosen the cabin because she'd loved the freedom and wide-open space it provided, and it had a fireplace. The outdoorsy feel and somewhat rustic living appealed to her. Having lived in the city much of her life she'd been excited at the prospect of having a home in the quiet solitude of the woods. When she'd viewed the cabin for the first time, Ariana had known instantly she had to have it for her home.

"I appreciate your offer. It's very kind of you. But if it's all the same to you, I think I'd rather stay here."

"Do you truly think that's wise?" Bastion asked, not liking her response one bit, yet knowing instantly he wouldn't be able to change her mind.

"Wise or not, I will not be run off from my home again. I appreciate your offer to allow me out of my lease, Bastion. But what has become painfully obvious to me, is that I can no longer run from this," Ariana explained as emotion caused her throat to tighten. She hiccupped, and her eyes filled with despair. "This person followed me all the way from Massachusetts. If it must end, I'd rather it be here with me then for the stalker to go after someone else."

Sighing with regret, Bastion nodded his head in understanding. He turned to leave.

"Please, tell Kalabernus that I'm truly sorry he got sucked into this, as well as for any pain I may have caused him," Ariana called after Bastion, giving him reason to pause and turn back toward her.

"And why, Ariana, would you think you caused him pain?" Bastion asked quietly.

"He just..." Inhaling deeply Ariana fought back the tears attempting to spill forth anew. He had called her by her real name. It was clear they all knew everything - even who she really was. "Well, he just seemed so tortured last night when he left," she finished sadly with her head bowed.

"Tortured," Bastion repeated softly, staring at her intently. "My dear Ariana, torture doesn't even begin to cover his forty years of existence. I'll have a new lease drawn up for you with your corrected information. I trust everything else will stay the same?" Turning abruptly, he walked away, got into his vehicle and drove off moments later.

Chapter 7

Kalabernus leaned against a tree as he watched his father and Ariana from a distance. They stood at the doorway of his old cabin.

The place he'd once called home.

He knew from where they stood that he was thoroughly hidden from their view, so he was by no means worried about being seen. One thing the shadows had taught him quite well over the years was how to hide in plain sight or disappear into the shadowy recesses most couldn't see. The foliage in this location was dense and allowed for shadows to swoop in and out around him as they taunted him.

"They know!" Veranke hissed, cackling with glee. Swirling around Kalabernus the dark creature wrapped him in his inky black essence. "They all know what you did."

Tearing a branch off the tree in frustration he whacked it against the ground, becoming irritable at their incessant verbal onslaughts. The shadows had been tormenting him ruthlessly ever since he'd left Ariana the night before. He could only imagine the poison they were spewing into her ears, even now as she spoke with his father.

Looking back down at the cabin he growled deep in his throat as his eyes shifted around the clearing where the house sat. There was a presence now within the woods around the house.

Somewhere within, it was hiding.

He sensed its evil nature just as easily as he could feel the demonic shadows next to him. Unable to pinpoint the stalker's exact location, Kalabernus expected it was because the evil monster was being protected by shadows of his own. Whether the stalker was aware of that or not didn't matter to him. What did matter to him was that they appeared to be biding their time. And apparently, they and the stalker weren't done with their game. The note Kalabernus had found on his windshield upon coming out of the Sheriff's department, of all places, made that plainly clear. Peering down at the three by five card in his hand, he re-read the words printed neatly on it.

"The black-haired beauty was meant for me. Time to pay."

Crumpling the card in his hand, he shoved it into his pocket. His expression was fierce, his glowing pale blue eyes more pronounced by his dark hiding place and the shadows which haunted him. It was apparent to Kalabernus the stalker had other intentions for Ariana last night. The sick dirtbag had planned to be in her bed doing heaven only knows what to her, rather than Kalabernus. With the cabin being as secluded as it was, it might have been days, even weeks for that matter before anyone would have been aware of her absence and come looking.

Observing that his father and Ariana appeared to be finishing with their conversation as Bastion moved to walk away, Kalabernus grunted angrily. His father had no right to get involved but he suspected he knew why, nonetheless. When he'd insisted that Kalabernus move home and he'd tried to refuse, his dad had pointed out the deed hadn't been placed in his name yet. Which meant he didn't own it and had no rights to it, regardless of whether it had been his home, and his haven for several years.

He watched as Ariana headed back into the cabin admiring the way she looked in her tight jeans and a long-sleeved t-shirt. He remembered well how she had looked, how she'd felt in his arms. Closing his eyes, he rested his head against the tree trunk behind him, groaning with misery. He longed for such a life. A normal life. One where a woman wanted him regardless of his cursed state. He'd mistakenly allowed himself to fantasize for a brief time last night that he might be able to have it all. That he'd found a woman who might be able to see past that.

Snarling angrily, he flung the tree branch roughly away and bared his teeth, forcing his eyes to surreptitiously scan his surroundings. Witnessing movement down at the cabin he noted the garage door rising and the vehicle within drove slowly away.

One thing was for sure, Kalabernus thought, realizing Ariana was likely gone for the day. There was no way he was going to allow history to repeat itself. If the shadows, or even this stalker for that matter, believed they were going to make Ariana and him a pawn in another one of their games they were sadly mistaken. He knew what he had to do.

It had been a long time.

And he hadn't practiced for years.

Not since he'd been caught the last time by his father and told he needed to knock it off.

But as far as Kalabernus was concerned, if he was going to catch a monster, he'd have to become a demon.

- - -

Ariana was hungry. After Bastion left she investigated her cupboards and fridge, only to discover how completely lacking in provisions she was. Determining she'd need to go grocery shopping, she decided it was high time she fully stocked her pantry.

Being sure to double and triple check all her windows, patio doors and locks she additionally set about making traps in front of each entry point. They were slight and seemingly innocuous in nature, but she knew they would aid her in determining whether someone had entered her home in her absence. Shaking the last of the salt across the kitchen window ledge she tossed the empty container in the trash and brushed off her hands, making a mental note to pick up more at the store. Grabbing her purse and keys Ariana left through the door leading into the garage.

Ducking her head through first, she peered around the garage interior then ran to its back door, being sure to lock it. Propping a rake across its door handle she then peered into the back seat of her vehicle, popped and checked the interior of her trunk, then got into her car and promptly locked the doors. Checking her rearview mirror, she depressed the button for the garage door and it began to open.

Her heart thudded in her chest anxiously, wondering and worrying if something might jump out at her.

Nothing came.

Seeing only trees swaying in the gentle breeze and leaves fluttering down from their many branches, she took a deep breath and gripped her steering wheel.

"Here we go," she whispered as she backed out of the garage into the late morning light. Punching the garage door button quickly she crept slowly down the drive, periodically glancing in her rearview mirror, while at the same time paying close attention that nothing and no one entered her garage as the door came down.

Expelling a shaky breath of relief, she drove away, all the while struggling to keep from crying. Lips trembling Ariana fought back the tears threatening to spill forth down her cheeks. Feeling desperate over having to go through the same repetitive motions she had been having to endure for years now, Ariana banged at the wheel while heading into town. This was supposed to be her chance to start over fresh; a new state, a new home, a new name even. Being a freelance writer, she'd realized she could effectively work anywhere. Broaching the subject with several of her long-time clients within Massachusetts, they had all been more than willing to continue working with her from a distance.

Adjusting in her seat, Ariana rested her head against the cushion of her seat. What bothered her the most was that she'd potentially put other people at risk. Mistakenly believing she was now safe, she'd reached out to her long-time friend and college roommate, Angela Powers. Worried that her decision to come to Loveland, Colorado had been a mistake she banged her head against the headrest in frustration. She'd only been in Massachusetts for about a week and a half now, but she'd grown to love it here. She really liked being able to go out with her friend and have the freedom to meet new people without worrying and wondering if they were her stalker.

That thought brought her mind around to Kalabernus. Removing one hand from the steering wheel she depressed it against her belly, trying to ease the queasiness she was experiencing. Her memory from the night before was still foggy and the mild headache she was experiencing in its aftermath wasn't helping any. But bits and pieces were coming back to her.

He'd been so gentle with her. Of that she was certain. Ariana even had a vague recollection of being pulled from the hot tub, not recalling when she'd gotten in. Suspecting he might well have saved her from a fate much worse than being drugged, she squeezed her eyes shut briefly, once again trying to quell her guilt at having put him in that position.

She wasn't stupid.

She knew full well that she was extremely attractive to men and had to be extra cautious of her responses with them because of it. She even made it a point not to wear revealing attire but that didn't seem to matter. Ariana could only imagine what she might have said or done to encourage him and knew it likely hadn't taken much to gain his interest.

Shaking her head to dispel her wandering thoughts Ariana made the conscious decision to not think about it for a while. Right now, she needed to eat. Then she'd head to the store for provisions as well as a few items she'd need to assist in her security around the house. Bastion wasn't wrong after all. Her home was secluded. For all she knew, her stalker had already staked it out when she first moved in over a week ago. She needed to be proactive.

With a pained grimace, she also realized she would need to stop into the Sheriff's department whether she liked it or not. Obviously, Sheriff RavenCroft was already aware of the stalker and his most recent prank. She suspected he'd likely requested the case files from Dalton, Massachusetts or Bastion wouldn't have known what her real name was already. Why, oh why, she thought, did the Sheriff of Loveland County have to be the brother of the man she had been intimate with the night before? And to learn she was renting from their father, Bastion RavenCroft, the home Kalabernus once lived in had been slightly unsettling. Somehow, she'd managed to entangle herself in an entire family's life and she hoped desperately it wouldn't end up destroying them all in the long run.

Arriving in town Ariana noticed a local coffee house while driving down the main street. Deciding to run in for coffee and a bite to eat she located an empty parking space between two brightly painted cars in a location void of trees not far from the shop. Being sure to lock her doors she paid close attention to her surroundings as well as other pedestrians as she crossed the street. Entering the coffee house, she waited patiently in a short line to order her drink and sandwich. She just reached the counter when the woman in front of her accidentally bumped into her as she was moving away with a bag and drink in hand.

"Oh, I'm so sorry!" the woman exclaimed. Still wearing sunglasses and sporting her hat and gloves with a long purple stadium parka fringed with faux fur, she appeared to be in a hurry.

"It's no problem. Really," Ariana replied quickly with a lazy smile.

The woman moved to leave then halted, turning back toward Ariana thoughtfully. Her medium length straight black hair swung around her shoulders as she turned.

"Might I recommend a tea rather than coffee today?" the woman suggested, gesturing toward the sign listing teas. "They have a rather nice mint tea that can help soothe bellies and jangled nerves," she stated. Then giving her a short nod, she strode away, taking a drink from her own coffee cup as she went.

Finding the exchange odd, Ariana stared up at the sign. Frowning, she realized she really wasn't in the mood for coffee. Eyeing the list of teas, she decided to go ahead and order the mint tea as suggested, wondering at how the woman had known of her anxiety. She wondered if it was really that obvious.

Taking her sandwich and tea to go, she requested directions to the Sheriff's department from the cashier before departing, figuring she'd probably better make that her first stop. Not knowing how long it would take, she didn't want her groceries sitting in the vehicle for very long, regardless of the cool weather outside.

As usual, Ariana stole cautious glances around her as she headed back to the car. The hairs on the back of her neck began to tingle from the sensation of being watched. Or was she simply being paranoid? Reaching her car, she realized with a chill that she wasn't. On her windshield, propped underneath the driver's side wiper was a round card with a note attached. Snatching it up she peered hastily around her, trying desperately to catch sight of who it might have been. No one had been near it as she'd left the coffee house, she was sure of it. Her car had been visible from the entrance of the building.

"Excuse me," she called to a woman passing nearby, gaining her attention. "Did you happen to see who might have left this?"

Shaking her head and giving her a funny look, the woman moved on, barely mumbling a response. "No, sorry."

Hands shaking, Ariana cringed then peered down at the paper and card in her hand. The circular card had a large heart shape drawn around her face with an X across it.

"*Should have never cheated. There will be retribution for all,*" the note read.

Chest heaving in distress as panic and terror surged within her, Ariana began to cry.

- - -

Retribution?

Oh, boy, that doesn't sound good at all.

I don't know about you, but I'm betting that this threat of retribution isn't going to go over well with Kalabernus and his family when they find out about it. The RavenCrofts, if you haven't noticed already, are a tight-knit family who are not likely to stand by while someone attempts to dole out their own personal form of punishment on one of their family members over a non-existent crime. At least, not if they can help it. Nor will they put up with an innocent woman like Ariana, a victim if you will, being threatened and terrorized. But of course, she doesn't know that yet, so the notion that she, or anyone else for that matter, could get hurt because of her is distressing her something fierce.

On a sidebar here, I must ask. How does this dim-witted stalker figure she's cheating anyway? Obviously, this guy is delusional which makes him that much more dangerous. From personal experience, I can tell you that when someone is crazy, their actions are that much more volatile and harder to track. There's just no telling what this guy's next move might be. If he was willing to take the life of Ariana's roommate, what do you suppose he's gonna do if he gets ahold of her?

To think that all of this started with what seemed an innocent admirer with a crush. The first note she ever received from her pursuer had been on the windshield of her car. A couple of weeks later there was another one. After about three months' worth of messages, Ariana thought she'd figured out who it was and had approached them while leaving work one day. But after an extremely embarrassing conversation, she quickly discovered the man was not her admirer and the co-worker strongly advised her to take it to the police. So, she did, and they started an investigation. The problem with these sorts of cases is that there's not much the police can really do. They can investigate an individual if they think they know who the stalker is, but when the perpetrator isn't known they're that much harder to pin down.

Over a span of about a year the messages began coming more frequently, we're talking three or four times a month and sometimes she would receive cards. The content within just kept getting darker and darker so her unease grew with each passing day. Instead of fun little quips or romantic poetic missives, the person would rant about the clothes she wore and tell her in detail all the things he wanted to do to her. The explicit accounts of the demented individual's daydreams about Ariana are how the police figured out that it was likely a male chasing her. If you get what I mean.

Pretty scary stuff, if you ask me.

Evidently, this so-called admirer had developed an extremely unhealthy obsession.

In some warped way, I suppose the lunatic thought he had a dating relationship with Ariana. But let's just be real for a minute here. If you like someone then you man up (or woman up as the case may be) and tell them. You don't leave them harassing missives on a weekly basis.

Hello!

As the years progressed her stalker began getting increasingly bothersome. That's right, I said years. The frequency of his notes to her escalated even further, sometimes even as many as four or five times a week. I'm sure you can imagine it caused Ariana to become paranoid about everyone she met. Soon she was receiving wilted flowers on her doorstep or they'd be sent to her work. The messages also became more demanding and controlling as if trying to eliminate her interaction with other people. Somehow her appointments were being changed, dates were getting canceled for her, and cruel messages and gifts were being left for friends who tried to help and suitors.

What was also troubling was that some of her close friendships and business relationships were being threatened by the stalker's jealous tactics. Any attempt she'd make to build upon her friendships or attempt to date was thwarted by her pursuer who would find some way to ruin things for her. Things had gotten so bad that in the last year she'd become a hermit. Ariana found herself taking more and more of her client work home to avoid co-workers and prevent her from having to leave her home because she constantly felt like she was being followed. After a while, the apartment she shared with her roommate had felt more like a prison than it did a haven.

No doubt the tears she now shed were from the misery of knowing that the person chasing her was now furious with both her and likely Kalabernus too. She knew she had to find a way to protect him because regardless of what had happened between them, no one deserved the kind of life-ending wrath her pursuer doled out. Problem was, nothing she'd done before had helped her to keep Kami safe. What could she possibly do to keep him from getting hurt too?

Chapter 8

He shouldn't have made her cry.

Pounding on his steering wheel Kalabernus fumed at having arrived too late. He'd managed to locate Ariana in time to see her crossing the street toward her car. Witnessing her reaction to the message she'd found on her vehicle Kalabernus seethed inwardly. It had taken him too long to get back to his vehicle from where he'd been hiding near the cabin. The question on his mind now, was how had her stalker gotten ahead of him?

Grateful to see her being cautious and checking her vehicle thoroughly before getting in, he gritted his teeth. Ariana shouldn't have to go to such measures to feel safe. Tapping on the seat next to him he became thoughtful. He'd seen his sister Synedra walking down Main Street toward her shop as he'd driven in. Her Herbal shop sat right next to her husband Nathan's detective agency. Debating on what he wanted to do, he opted instead for the moment to follow Ariana first. Whatever message the pursuer had relayed had been clearly upsetting, and he wanted to make sure she was okay.

After several minutes he realized she was heading in the direction of the Sheriff's department. Smart girl, he thought. Regardless of how awkward it might be for her, he was glad to see she wasn't disregarding the note. Seeing her pull in and get out, he pulled slowly past the parking lot, making sure she made it to the front door okay. Then, increasing his speed, he drove quickly around the block, heading back toward his brother-in-law's detective agency. He had a few questions and figured Nathan would be the best person to gain the answers he needed.

- - -

Taking a deep breath Ariana pulled open the glass door of the Sheriff's Department and found herself standing in a small waiting room. The walls were oak wood paneling and the matching two-seater chairs in the lobby area were covered in royal blue upholstery with varnished wood making up the arms and legs. A framed landscape of the local Rocky Mountains hung upon the wall above one of the chairs and a tall faux Ficus tree stood between the second chair and the receiving desk.

"I'd like to officially report a stalker," Ariana informed the officer seated behind the desk. She noted the deputy Sheriff's badge listed his name as deputy

Sheriff Mark Soder as he leaned back in his office chair and rocked back and forth in his seat. He gave her a shrewd look as if attempting to gauge her validity.

"Yes, ma'am. I'll need to get some information from you," Deputy Sheriff Soder replied finally, trying hard to keep from ogling the woman.

"Of course. Just so you know, it's a long drawn out case stemming from Dalton, Massachusetts. I believe you'll find Sheriff RavenCroft is already aware of the situation. But I've had a recent incident, you see, so..."

Hearing shouting erupting from the far office in the back of the room Ariana realized she recognized the voice. Both she and the deputy glanced toward the noise.

"What makes you think I'd ever let him back in my life, Kalturek? And how dare you attempt to match-make!" Angela was exclaiming fiercely as she rushed from the Sheriff's office. Followed out by a harried man with auburn hair and a seriously vexed Kalturek on their heels, she spun around and confronted them both. "I don't care who this guy thinks he is, he's not gonna scare me into letting Heaton back into my house for any length of time, period!" she insisted while gesturing wildly toward the man before her called Heaton. The individual in question wore black jeans and tennis shoes with a white muscle shirt. At five foot ten Heaton was by no means tall but he had the build of a fighter and well-defined muscular arms. His fluid gate gave the impression of a man who was more than capable of taking care of himself.

"I get that you guys are on the outs right now, Angela. The point I'm trying to make is that I just don't have the resources right now to put a twenty-four-hour guard on you and we both know you can't afford to hire a bodyguard," Kalturek responded, attempting to defend his suggestion.

"You'd be better off sending him down to guard Marcy Lou!" she argued back. "We all know that's where Heaton really wants to be."

Heaton groaned, rolling his eyes heavenward.

At the same time, Kalturek pursed his lips irritably and gestured toward Angela while waving at her with the paper he had in his hand. "Marcy Lou isn't the one in danger here. *You* are!"

"How serious is it with this guy?" Heaton asked, scowling toward Kalturek. He had the look of a man both confused and concerned all rolled into one.

The Sheriff shoved the paper toward Heaton. Taking it from him, Heaton let out a startled yelp after looking at it, causing the deputy's in their cubicles who weren't already listening in, to turn in surprise.

Clearly astonished by his reaction as well, Angela's shoulders sagged. "Look, Heaton…"

"*No, Angela,*" Heaton practically roared, his head shaking wildly from side to side. "*Are you kidding me with this?* Have you seen this? Have you seen what this stalker did to this woman?" Turning back towards Sheriff RavenCroft he asked, "Who was she to this friend of Angela's, Kalturek?"

The way they were all responding to each other, Ariana realized the people arguing had likely known each other for years.

"She was her roommate," Kalturek supplied, catching sight of Ariana out of the corner of his eye.

"*Her roommate?*" Heaton exclaimed in horror, whirling about in order to confront her. His voice rose as his panic became quite evident to all present. Swearing he continued to yell. "*Woman!* When are you gonna get it in your head that I don't give a crap about Marcy Lou? But I swear if anything ever happens to you... If this guy manages to get his hands on you..." Heaton dropped suddenly down on his knees in front of Angela. Wrapping his arms around her waist he pulled her close and held her tightly as he spoke, his voice charged with emotion. "Baby, please. *Please, baby, please!* You gotta let me back home." Voice trailing off he practically sobbed into her belly, his hands roaming around her hips then desperately wrapping her in his arms again.

Stunned and thoroughly touched by Heaton's reaction, Angela's eyes grew wide with embarrassment. She was still completely oblivious to the onlooker in the entryway as her back was to her.

"Oh, Heaton," Angela said finally, her expression changing suddenly from anger and resentment to tenderness. "Well, I... I guess I could make an exception for the time being," she stammered softly. Her hands cupped the back of his head as she gazed at him with affection. Her dishwater blonde hair hung haphazardly about her face in loose waves as it was falling out of her pony-tale. She'd obviously left the house in a hurry for she was not normally prone to appearing so frazzled.

Heaton peered hopefully up at her. Getting up from the floor, he continued to hold her. "Really? I'll sleep on the couch, I promise. I'll stay out of your way and even be sure to put the toilet seat down," he said urgently, clearly not caring that he was humbling himself before her.

"I think we can work those details out later," Angela said with a giggle. Her eyes lit up with a bemused smile.

Sheriff Kalturek RavenCroft watched as the couple laughed nervously together, and then turned to leave.

"No need to worry. I'll take really good care of her," Heaton called as he glanced back at the Sheriff.

Shaking his head while trying to suppress a chuckle, Kalturek crossed his arms over his chest. "No doubt in my mind that you will."

Catching sight of Ariana standing in the entryway as they were heading out, Angela and Heaton paused at the swinging door.

Overwhelmed with despair at having been the cause of so much trouble for her friend, Ariana's face scrunched up. Angry tears welled in her eyes. Locking gazes with Heaton she gave him an apologetic look. "I'm so sorry." Her voice was small, even to her own ears.

"No worries. I got this," Heaton assured her, recognizing that Ariana was the one the stalker was likely after in the first place.

Tentatively, Angela tried to get her friends attention, noting that she wouldn't even look at her. "Ariana, please. Let me…"

"No," Ariana said firmly. "Just don't. Stay away from me right now," she insisted, becoming more and more angry at herself. Tears were streaming down her cheeks and she couldn't seem to stop them.

Deftly maneuvering Angela away, Heaton assisted her out of the Sheriff's Department. Making his way out first, he scanned his surroundings quickly, then urged Angela along with him.

"Ariana Davis, I presume? Not Sareena?" Sheriff Kalturek RavenCroft said quietly, having watched the exchange with difficulty.

"Yes. Sareena was my sister," Ariana admitted truthfully, her wet lashes blinking away tears. Extending her hand toward him she proffered the notecard she received. "I received another one and figured you should know," she said, trying hard to appear calm and angry, rather than terrified.

But she couldn't fool him.

"When?" He took several strides toward her and propped open the swinging door to let her into the offices.

"A few minutes ago. I was coming out of the coffee house."

"Which one?"

"Downtown off Main Street."

Taking the circular card and paper from her, he read the message the stalker had left behind. He looked sharply up at her. "I'll get a deputy to…"

"It won't do any good," Ariana spouted furiously. "He's been after me for over five years. You think I haven't been through all this before? You think the police in Dalton didn't do all the same things you're thinking to do now?" She'd come awful close to shouting, having become desperate and increasingly outraged at the situation. She stood there shaking before him. "In the end, it didn't do any good."

"Please don't give up. There are things I can do to protect you."

"Things you can do? And what about the people around me? Angela for example. Or your brother for that matter," she said, garnering his attention. "Somehow this guy knows what happened last night. He's clearly even more pissed off now than he was before. Sheriff RavenCroft, if this guy is mad at *me*, then just imagine what he might do to Kalabernus."

"You're actually afraid for my brother?" Kalturek asked, more than a little puzzled by her concern. He noted his deputies were intently eavesdropping.

"Why wouldn't I be? He's innocent in this. He did nothing wrong."

"I see," he said slowly, giving her a quizzical look. "I can assure you, Kalabernus is more than capable of taking care of himself."

"That's what Kami thought too, and she was well versed in martial arts. When someone wants to kill you, they're usually pretty good at finding a way." Ariana could see her statement had troubled him and it left behind an uncomfortable silence.

Kalturek's cheek twitched as he contemplated the woman before him, attempting to determine what he might be able to say to give her some peace of mind. "I appreciate your concern for my brother. It's more than most would give him. But if we're gonna be completely honest here, I think this stalker should be more afraid of my brother."

"You don't know this stalker the way I do. He's eluded the police for almost five years now. He's cocky, manipulative, and tricky."

"You don't know my brother the way I do. He's scary as hell. Most of my deputies won't admit it, but not even they want to meet him in a dark alley."

"What does that mean?" Ariana inquired, perplexed by the Sheriff's opinion of his brother.

"Let's just talk about your safety right now. All right?"

"What's the point?" Ariana said, not bothering to walk through the opened swinging door he was holding for her. Instead, she began to walk away.

"Ariana, *wait!*" Kalturek called almost crossly, becoming peeved by her unwillingness to cooperate.

"Sheriff RavenCroft, I'm not stupid. Look what happened to my friend Kami. I know how this ends," Ariana choked out. Stiffening her posture with resolve she turned her wounded expression from him and walked away, disappearing through the entrance doors.

Swearing fiercely Sheriff Kalturek RavenCroft slammed the swinging door shut, busting it from its hinges.

Chapter 9

Already tired after what felt like a very long day, Ariana was not really in the mood to be grocery shopping. Recognizing the need to have food in the house, however, she made her way to the grocery store and began filling her cart, not particularly paying attention too much to what she was grabbing.

"If I'm not careful I'm going to wind up spending a thousand dollars on groceries," she muttered to herself while scanning the aisle signs for snack foods and chips. Catching sight of the correct aisle she headed in that direction. If it looked like something she normally kept in the house, she tossed it in the cart. After a while, she realized her cart was starting to fill up quickly and she couldn't figure out why. It felt like she hadn't even started to fill her pantry yet since she'd only been through a couple aisles.

Moving along at a brisk pace she continued to snatch up her favorite bags of crunchy snacks then headed for the frozen foods section. Not paying attention to where she was going, she rammed her cart into someone who was attempting to quickly disappear down another aisle.

"I'm so sorry. I guess I'm in my own little world," Ariana said quickly. Looking up at the man she'd run into her mouth dropped and she lost all train of thought. Staring back at her was Kalabernus RavenCroft. He was wearing what looked like camouflage pants and a hunter green shirt while carrying a dark jacket over his shoulder. And he looked really good too.

"N...no need to apologize. Imagine you got an awful lot on your mind," Kalabernus said quietly. His gaze flitted about the store anxiously, his crystal-clear blue eyes appearing to almost glow eerily. He had such a strikingly handsome look about him and yet somehow, even in the bright light of the store, he seemed to have a brooding countenance. There was a five o'clock shadow along his jaw and chin, making him appear even more intimidating. She couldn't help thinking it made him that much more appealing.

"Yes, well..." Ariana's voice trailed off, and she found she didn't know quite what to say. "I received another note," she said finally, wishing she hadn't said anything and wondering why in the world she'd said that in the first place.

Kalabernus's eyes softened on her. "I got me one too. It would seem we've joined the same club," he responded, shaking the crumpled card in his hand before her. Seeing her agitated and distressed reaction to it he swore aloud. "No worries. Nothing I can't handle," he reassured darkly.

"Your brother seemed to think the same thing."

"My brother?" His brow rose questioningly.

"Sheriff RavenCroft," Ariana supplied.

"Oh, right, Kalturek."

Ariana fidgeted. Glancing away awkwardly her gaze shifted back and their eyes met.

"Do you wanna...?"

"I'm sorry I..."

They spoke over the top of each other, and then each stopped at the same time. Smiling nervously up at Kalabernus, Ariana giggled. He scowled, his arm swiping over his shoulder at something. For the briefest second, Ariana imagined she saw a grayish cloud hovering above his shoulder. Her head tilted, and she frowned curiously, thinking that had been a funny notion.

"You were asking something?" Kalabernus asked finally, knowing he probably looked and sounded like an idiot. The three most bothersome shadows whom he often referred to as 'the troublesome three' had taken it upon themselves to follow him through the store, trying to bait him at every turn. He'd been attempting to watch her from a distance, to see if he could catch sight of anyone following her. But the shadows had been hindering him in his endeavor.

"I just thought... Would you like to join me for dinner?" she asked, surprising both of them. Where in the world had that come from?

"You want... You want I join you for dinner?" Kalabernus asked in astonishment causing her to blush.

She stammered. "Well, I guess... I mean... I sort of figure it's the least I could do, fix you dinner that is. You know, considering..." Ariana paused, unsure what was possessing her to keep talking, or for that matter, invite him back to the cabin again. The man probably thought she was nuts. She knew she should be turning tail and running but for some reason, she felt drawn to him instead. There was a lost, little boy quality to him that she found endearing.

Scratching at his jaw, Kalabernus eyed her curiously, dumbfounded by her offer. If anything, he figured it was just the opposite, that he owed her dinner, and so much more. Shrugging, trying to give off the appearance of nonchalance, he poked into her basket.

"Well, I guess that depends," he said finally.

"On?"

"What are you making?" He gave her a devilish look. "All I see here are boxes of ding-dongs and ho-ho's, bags of chips, crackers, and cookies."

Ariana blinked. Had she filled her cart with nothing but junk food? She never ate like that. Peering into her cart with a look of bewilderment on her face Kalturek chuckled.

"Mind you, I like me some junk food but, you know, meat is good too. The occasional vegetable and potato, or pasta even can really round out a meal."

Ariana grinned back at him and he smiled.

She melted.

Sensing someone coming up behind her she glanced back apologetically, realizing they were blocking their way.

"I'm so sorry. Where's my head?" Attempting to scoot the cart over unsuccessfully, she watched in awe as Kalabernus lifted it easily and set it down closer to the shelves with Mexican food.

"Poison. Give him poison," the shadowy demon Veranke crooned in her ear.

Overhearing the shadow, Kalabernus scowled again, then watched as Ariana rubbed the same ear harshly as if she'd been tickled.

"Mexican," she said absentmindedly a second later.

"Sorry?"

"I can make tacos." Grabbing a box of hard taco shells from the shelf next to her, she also randomly swiped a jar of salsa along with a bag of flour tortillas and a can of refried beans.

"You sure...you sure you want my company?" he stuttered in amazement, feeling a bit at loose ends. He didn't know quite what to make of her offer.

"Better the devil I don't know than the one I do, I figure." She responded without thinking while pushing the cart toward the meat section of the store; she needed hamburger. Catching sight of several shoppers peering her way, Ariana noted that for some reason, they seemed to be gaining the attention of people around them. She couldn't quite figure out why. Realizing suddenly what she'd just said and that he wasn't following her anymore, Ariana stopped and looked back.

"Kalabernus, I'm so sorry. I didn't mean to imply..."

"No, you're right. I am a devil," he insisted quietly. His expression was one of pain as he moved toward her. "Everybody knows it. That's why they're staring, you see? Cause I'm a giant, intimidating and scary. And I...well, I exude a kind of dangerous vibe. You know what I mean? Because of that, they're wondering how you can possibly want to have anything to do with me, let alone talk to me. Frankly, I'm wondering the same thing, particularly after what I did to you last night." He whispered the last quietly, so others couldn't hear. His hauntingly beautiful eyes searched her face.

Ariana moved towards him, standing so close she had to peer up to look into his eyes. "Have you ever read the Bible?"

"Some." He scratched at his jaw again. It occurred to him he needed a shave. "I never put much stock in it though," he answered honestly.

"So, you've read about Satan?"

"A bit," he responded, unsure of what she was getting at. He hadn't read the Bible since his childhood. That was way back when he'd gone searching for answers to his cursed state but never got any. "He was also known as Lucifer as I understand it."

"Yes, and a devil. If you know that, then you might also know…that even the devil is an angel. Though a fallen one at that. Are you?"

"Am I what?" He was confused, and she had him all tied up in knots inside. He didn't like that. Not one bit and he most certainly didn't know what to make of it.

"A fallen angel."

"I've never been accused of being an angel of any kind," Kalabernus drawled humorously. "I'm too scary."

Harrumphing softly Ariana walked back to her cart, forcing him to follow. "You aren't scary. Trust me, because I've known real fear. I'd take your kind of scary any day."

Unbeknownst to her, Kalabernus smiled.

- - -

Does that seem unnatural to you or what?

In any situation I've ever come across, where a woman had been wronged by a man in an intimate way, regardless of the reasons, the woman never wanted to have any further contact with him. The usual mindset is that they'd rather not be reminded of the incident. And yet, here Ariana is, not only talking amiably with Kalabernus but, inviting him back to her home for dinner.

Or rather, his home.

No, wait, technically it's owned by Bastion. Kalabernus only ever lived there.

Anyway...

Looking back, I've always wondered about this. But then, I've come to believe over time that for individuals like Kalabernus, who can see these shadowy creatures, there are very few who are likely capable of understanding them. You know? People with the tolerance, patience, and understanding of the darkness which plagues them. I'd posit to say that it takes someone who has experienced and lived with or endured such darkness to be able to be sympathetic to them.

Hhhmmm. Almost makes you wonder where this is going, don't it?

In either event, things are about to get a little more interesting. So, pay close attention to what's about to happen next.

- - -

Following her back to the cabin in his truck, Kalabernus assisted Ariana in bringing her groceries inside. Shaking out of their jackets, he tossed them in the living room chair then began unpacking her things.

Helping to put her things away was almost surreal to him. He'd gotten groceries before on his own and had even assisted with it on numerous occasions in his father's home. But somehow it was different doing the chore with her.

Finishing putting everything away, they both stopped and stared at each other.

"So ... what now?" Kalabernus asked awkwardly.

Ariana looked at her clock. "It's almost five. I could start dinner."

They peered around the kitchen and laughed at the same time.

"I suppose it would have made more sense leaving out what we needed," Kalabernus teased.

Working together they managed to pull all the required ingredients back out and began setting about preparing dinner. The conversation stemmed mostly around preparation. Before long they had a dozen 'double-decker taco's,' as Kalabernus called them, sitting on a long tray on the breakfast counter. Carrying tall glasses of milk around the counter, Ariana sat down on a bar stool next to him and set one down before each of them.

"That's a lot of food." She stared at the platter with widening eyes, thinking they looked awfully good. She liked his suggestion of wrapping crunchy tacos in small flour tortillas spread with refried beans.

Kalabernus looked at her, then laughed. The sound was rich and hearty, and she sensed he didn't make the noise often which for some reason made her want to cry.

"That? Oh, well, that's just a snack." His crystal-clear blue eyes sparkled with amusement as he smiled.

Returning the laugh, she became so worked up that she snorted into her napkin, inciting even more laughter on his part.

"She's beautiful and she snorts too. Who would have ever guessed," he said while placing four tacos on his plate to start.

Chatting amiably about several newfound common interests, they soon finished eating and began cleaning up the kitchen.

"I just realized," Ariana said suddenly, as she rinsed their plates in the sink. "I was supposed to cook *you* dinner. You weren't supposed to help me."

He turned to her, a mischievous look in his eye. "I guess that means you still owe me dinner?" he asked almost hopefully, though he'd meant it as more of a statement.

Laughing, she grabbed the dish towel and tossed it at him. "Maybe I should make you cook me dinner." Then suddenly her expression changed. Face draining of color she turned back toward the patio door. Standing on the other side of the glass was the faceless black shape of a man. Its posture was that of one attempting to see inside.

Scritch, scratch.

It tapped on the window, like nails on a chalkboard, or in this case, glass.

Becoming alarmed by Ariana's horrified expression, Kalabernus followed her gaze. "What's the matter?"

"Kalabernus?" she stammered, her throat constricting from fear. "Is there a man on the back patio there?"

Scritch, scratch.

The figure continued to tap on the glass door.

"No, just shadows I'd imagine. Why? Did you hear something?" he inquired, thoroughly confused.

"So, you don't see anyone on the patio there?"

"There's no man or woman that I can see." Kalabernus insisted, becoming troubled by her ghostly pallor. All he could see was the shadow, Veranke, attempting to taunt him further by scraping his long, taloned fingers against the glass. Moments later he was joined by Fallon and Zalman. They each seeped in through the door, their greenish black inky essences floating like shapeless clouds across the ceiling toward them.

Ariana jumped at the sight of the frightening creatures slipping through the glass door and coming at her. Eyes wide with fright she elicited a high pitch squeal. Shrinking towards Kalabernus she leaned into him as though for protection.

"Are you okay?" Kalabernus asked, becoming increasingly concerned. The blasted dang 'troublesome three' had to show up now, of all times, he thought. He figured their presence was probably what was setting her off.

"I g...guess I'm just s...spooked from everything with the stalker." The black cloudy substance hovered above her dining room table, reaching out toward her as though calling to her. Shoving her face into his chest she huddled next to him, afraid to look back. Her eyes had to be playing a trick on her.

"Hey, it's okay. I got you. Nothing is going to harm you. Not while I'm around anyway."

Tilting his head forward, he nuzzled his chin against the top of her head. She smelled of wildflowers and honey. Wrapping her with one arm he reached out with another and angrily swiped toward the shadows, trying to beg them off. If he didn't know better, she almost acted as if she could see them. But he knew that wasn't possible. No one had ever been able to see them but him.

Feeling unusually chilled for some reason, Ariana clung to Kalabernus. He was so warm, and it felt good being in his arms. For the past hour or so the feeling within the kitchen had been relaxed and homey. But now the air seemed almost charged with menace, and it was setting her on edge.

And those things she was seeing.

What were they, she wondered?

She was afraid to look back.

"Don't go," she said suddenly, hating that she was being such a coward.

"You want... you want that I stay awhile?" he asked, trying to understand exactly what it was she was asking.

"Just stay and hold me," Ariana begged. Lifting her head briefly she glanced out of the corner of her eye toward the ceiling. A bright white light suddenly shimmered into view, like a flash from a camera. The black cloud skittered away, its black tentacle-like wisps moving along the ceiling toward the living room.

Kalabernus captured her face in his large beefy hands. His touch was tender, his tough skin feeling strong and capable against her smooth cheeks.

"Are you sure?" His voice was quiet, holding a hopeful note, but his clear blue eyes held a mixture of wanting and worry.

"I know I have no right to ask this of you, but I really just don't want to be alone. If you could just h...hold me for a while maybe..."

Kalabernus captured her lips, halting any further speech. Kissing her tenderly he groaned. Wanting so much more, but sensing she simply needed comfort, he lifted her into his arms. He moved toward the living room, but she stopped him. Her hands shook against his chest as she spoke.

"No, not the living room. Please, I...I can't." She didn't understand what she was seeing and didn't want to be in the same room with it.

"All right then."

He carried her through the kitchen and down the hall. Taking her into the bedroom, he lay her in bed and pulled off her shoes. At her gentle prompting, he crawled into bed next to her after kicking off his own footwear. Unsure of what he should do he felt her scoot up next to him, so he wrapped his arms around her, pulling her in closer to him. He could feel her trembling and didn't understand why, but for the moment he wasn't going to ask any questions for fear of ruining his chances at more time with her.

Chapter 10

"**W**here in the world have you been?"

Tensing, Kalabernus turned toward his brother Kahner who was coming down the stairs into the entryway. Having just arrived home mid-morning the next day, he groaned inwardly while rolling his eyes. He was, forty years old, and yet it felt like he was being treated like a teenager. Shoes in hand, he stood near the doorway, attempting the appearance of nonchalance rather unsuccessfully. He really wasn't in the mood for this confrontation.

"What's it to you?"

"Are you an idiot?"

"Well, let's see. My aptitude scores always tested higher than yours. So, what do you think?"

"Do you have any idea what you put Dad through last night? You never came home," Kahner accused, only slightly irritated by the reminder of his lower test scores.

"So? I've done that before. I'm not some stupid kid anymore. Who cares?"

Snorting loudly Kahner opened the top drawer of the stand in the entryway. Pulling out a circular card and a three-by-five index card, he shoved it into Kalabernus's hand.

"Dad ran out for pizza last night. He found that on the windshield of his vehicle when he came back out of Laynie's Pizza Emporium."

Staring down at the round card Kalabernus was astounded to see a picture of his face on it, with a giant red X crossing him out. It looked like it might have been taken as he was coming out of the grocery store with Ariana.

The index card read, "Even David managed to slay Goliath. The bigger they are, the harder they fall."

Growling loudly, Kalabernus crumpled the card and flung them to the floor. He'd been worried about leaving Ariana alone that morning when he left her house after breakfast. She'd seemed better when they first woke cuddled up together, but then at breakfast, she'd gotten spooked again. Concerned for her, he'd offered to stay longer. She'd looked like she wanted him to stay, but had, in the end, insisted she was fine and that he should head home. Now he was really wishing he hadn't left.

"Dad thought you might have attempted to go after this guy." Kahner gave him an accusing look. He waited impatiently for a response.

None came.

"Well, did you?"

Swearing Kalabernus scowled. "No, not last night. But after this I sure as heck will be!" he declared.

"Then, where were you?" Bastion asked, strolling down the hallway from the kitchen carrying two mugs in hand. He handed one off to Kahner who thanked him and took a drink.

Kalabernus didn't respond.

Bastion groaned and rolled his eyes. "You were at the cabin with Ariana, weren't you? I should have known." He shook his head in disgust.

"Even if I was, it's none of your business. And for your information she was scared. Seemed unnerved by something. Probably cause of this stalker of hers, and frankly, I don't blame her. So, I stayed with her."

Kahner's brow rose in response. "Stayed with her, eh?"

"Would you get your head out of the gutter?" Kalabernus flared. "I held her okay? I just...well...I held her is all." His tone was defensive.

"He's telling the truth," Drayke called from the hallway, coming into view. "See now, if it were me I would have..."

"You would have what?" Laynie blustered, following on his heels behind him. Stamping her feet on the floor she fisted her hands on her hips as she glared at her husband. The RavenCroft brothers and their father had been talking all morning about how beautiful Ariana Davis was. It had been making Laynie more than just a little jealous.

"I would have given her a sleeping pill and gone home to my beautiful, sexy, and loving wife," Drayke said quickly, eliciting a chuckle from the men.

"Too little, too late," Bastion mumbled with a smirk, then sipped at his coffee. His eyes twinkled merrily. His son Drayke was forever getting in trouble with his wife, Laynie.

"You got that right," Laynie fumed. "Consider yourself cut-off for a while," she declared, throwing daggers at Drayke with her eyes. Sashaying her hip, she turned with a scowl and stalked back to the kitchen.

"Wait, Baby! How long is a while?" Drayke shouted after her in despair.

"I'll let you know," she shouted back.

Grinning at each other, Kalabernus and Kahner exchanged humorous looks with their father.

"Don't worry, Laynie will forget. She usually does... Doesn't she?" Bastion asked after a brief pause.

"Oh, no," Drayke said, shaking his head seriously. "Your daughter, my twin sister mind you, thought it would be a good idea to get Laynie an iPad for her birthday. No thanks to Mackenzie, my wife's been keeping track of when she cuts me off now, through the calendar on it."

"Your very welcome," Mackenzie could be heard to say. Coming into the living room from the kitchen doorway with a grin on her face, she stopped suddenly, her expression changing drastically as she stared at Kalabernus.

"What's wrong with you? Something about you is different," Mackenzie said. Reaching toward him she touched his forehead. "Are you feeling okay?" she asked further, sensing an unusual vibe from him.

"Leave him alone, Mackenzie," Sable said softly, descending the stairs towards them. "He's got, someone…well, someone that he cares about on his mind is all." She paused tactfully as she spoke. Sable's eyes sparkled as she sidled up to her husband Kahner.

Understanding dawned on Mackenzie instantly. Wailing loudly as she shook the hand she'd touched her brother with wildly, she walked quickly away. "Oh, Lord have mercy! I don't need to know when you're feeling that!" she cried.

Becoming increasingly uncomfortable with the direction of the conversation, Kalabernus dropped his shoes where he stood and headed upstairs. "I think I'll go change my clothes," he said quickly as he disappeared.

Bastion laughed, then groaned. "Oh, man! That boy has got it bad." Swearing, he tilted his mug to his lips and disappeared down the hall towards his study. He had a bad feeling he knew full well what that was gonna mean.

- - -

They were everywhere.

She couldn't get away from them.

Whirling before her like monstrous shrieking demons, their glowing blood red eyes glared fiercely at her. Attempting to crawl away from them across the carpeted floor of her living room, Ariana whimpered as she trembled. What was happening to her? Was she going crazy?

Wishing now that she hadn't told Kalabernus it was okay to leave that morning, she wondered briefly what he would have been able to do if he'd stayed until this evening when the shadows showed up again. She'd swung at them when they first made their presence known, but they simply cackled with glee. Her attempts were clearly useless for her arms simply cut through them like a hot knife to melting butter.

"Go away! Get away from me!"

"He's gonna get you my pretty," Zalman crooned, swirling up around her shoulder. The closer he came the colder she felt at his presence as if she would never feel warmth again.

"He'll cut you! *He'll tear you!*" shrieked the demon Fallen, who hovered mercilessly before her, enjoying their game.

"*He'll rip you to pieces!*" Veranke growled fiercely. Gnashing his jowls, the creature stretched its fleshless black slithering arms toward her.

She screamed in terror.

Outside her patio door, the figure watched in wonder at the sight of the woman shrieking and screaming on her living room floor. He could see her hunkered down between the chair and couch, cowering in fear from some unseen force. Confused by her behavior the dark figure took satisfaction in seeing her in distress, nonetheless. Was it possible he had managed to succeed, he thought? Had he finally stripped her down? Could it be she was ready for him?

Yes, he was sure of it.

The voices in his head told him so.

Soon, not today, but soon he would have her. She would be his and he'd never let her go.

Ariana Davis was supposed to have been his already. He'd planned for it to happen when he'd slipped her the drink at the bar, but his chance had been ripped away by the giant RavenCroft man. The dark figure slammed his hand angrily against the glass patio door. The sound elicited another frightened cry from Ariana and he took pleasure in her fear.

He chuckled gleefully.

"That's right you witch. No one cheats on me," he said aloud, his lips curling into a grotesque smile.

He had been working for this, striving for this moment for so long. He'd nearly been stopped when he'd first begun this path once many, many years before. Her sister Sareena had discovered about him and tried to stop him. She was going to tell on him, she'd said but he'd taken care of her; silenced her as he did with the roommate many years later. Just like he would take care of this man now.

He was big, yes.

A little intimidating even.

But the voices told him he could be brought down. It was only a matter of time.

He could hear her crying and imagined the tears streaming down her cheeks. Adjusting his night vision goggles, he could see her scooting toward a stand. She grabbed the small box sitting on it and dug her hand desperately inside for her treasure within. Clasping it tightly in her hand she pulled it from the box and began talking. Or was she whispering? He couldn't tell for sure from where he was at but in the living room, the shadows could tell.

They screeched.

They howled.

They flung their arms about their faceless heads as though in pain.

Startled, Ariana peered up at the shadows now cowering away. A bright white light had flashed suddenly within the room between her and the dark shape-shifting figures, the moment she'd grabbed for the item from the box. The treasure had once belonged to her sister Sareena as a child, but she'd given it to Ariana when she started fifth grade. Sareena had been several years older than her, but they had always been close.

"Take it, Ariana. One day it will protect you. One day it will keep you safe from the darkness which seeks to harm you," her sister had said. She'd had a troubled look in her eye at the time. Was it possible that even then, somehow, Sareena had known someone would one day be after her?

Tears trickled down her cheeks at the memory. She'd thought it such an odd thing to say at the time, but now she understood.

"But sissy, you love it." Ariana remembered saying while trying to give it back. "He gave it to you when he pulled you from the water. I know how much it means to you."

"Yes, but you mean more to me. You haven't been in the water yet, so you need it more. It will protect you as long as you believe it will."

The white light was warm and inviting. It shifted protectively before her. Ariana continued to whisper fervently as she cried, holding it close to her heart. She stayed that way for a long time continuing to whisper the words her sister had taught her. After a while, her eyes began to droop as exhaustion set in and a troubled sleep took over.

- - -

Personally?

If it were me and I was seeing what she was seeing?

...I would... well, shoot...

...I'd wet myself!

There I said it. You happy now?

Man, wouldn't you!? Geezy-criminy and holy bacon-fritters. Wispy, greenish-black smoky creatures slithering through my patio door and along my ceiling toward me? The thought alone is enough to make me have an accident. Seriously, how does one fend off something like that?

Right about now, you might be wondering what the tarnation is going on here?

And how the heck is Ariana suddenly capable of being able to see the same shadows that Kalabernus has been seeing all his life? Right? One might conclude that the shadows can present themselves to someone they feel is a threat, so they can try and scare them away. But how could little ole' Ariana possibly be a threat to them?

Hhhmmm, let's think about this.

These loathsome, disgusting, vile, shadowy demonic bullies feed off our fears, our sorrows, our losses, and our sadness. If a woman were to come along and make Kalabernus happy? Fill him with joy and hope? They'd lose their snack, right? Of course, there could be something else going on here but what could that be? Hhhmmm?

By the way, did you catch that phrase?

The one Ariana made.

You know.

When she was recalling the memory of her sister Sareena, and she said…

"…When he pulled you from the water."

I won't lie, the first time I read those words a numbing sensation had washed over me. I even recall scoffing and thinking to myself, "Really? Did the author have to go there? Did they have to add religion to the story?"

Here's the funny thing about this.

Thus far in the RavenCroft's 'terrible' and 'trouble' filled tales both the original author, as well as the author of this book here, have been very adamant that the RavenCroft's were not religious people. Because of that, the tone of these stories would be more secular in nature. Bastion RavenCroft and his late wife Inara had never raised their children in church. It was a personal choice of course, and that was their right. No doubt about that.

But…

...just because the RavenCroft's aren't religious doesn't mean religion doesn't play a part in this tale. Or any other story, for that matter. Nor does it mean that other people within their lives are without faith.

At one point, early on in Ariana Davis's life, her family were avid churchgoers. Her parents attended church regularly making sure to bring along their daughters so that they could learn what Christianity was. They wanted them to be able to make an informed choice for themselves. Apparently, Ariana's big sister Sareena did just that. At fifteen years of age, Sareena Davis became a born-again Christian. As is the custom, her youth pastor baptized her in a ceremony at their church. After pulling Sareena from the water he'd given her a little token, or memory sake if you will. It was something for her to remember that moment, and that day, for the rest of her life. As stated, it meant a great deal to Sareena but for some reason, she gave it up to her eleven-year-old sister, Ariana.

Makes me wonder...

Think our young Sareena might have somehow known something we didn't?

Hhhhmmm. Honestly, at this point in the RavenCroft's story, I myself would have simply said it was a mere coincidence. As this family's story progresses, however, my opinion on such things changed and I've come to learn two very important things.

People come and go in our lives for a reason.

And ... there's no such thing as coincidence.

Chapter 11

Saw him he did, with his own two eyes.

The monster was real all right.

And most definitely a man.

Kalabernus sprinted across the forest. His sure-footed steps barely a whisper as they swiftly carried him up, over, and around the bushes, brush, and trees in his way. Most thought with his massive frame and height that he'd be clumsy and slow, oafish even. It was exactly the opposite. Well accustomed to his own size and how to maneuver his body quickly, he was more than capable of keeping the dark figure in sight. The only problem was catching up. He'd had a bit more of a head start then what Kalabernus cared for him to have.

Likely surprising Ariana's predator with how close he'd gotten, the man pelted from the patio decking where he'd been spying on her. His dark brown coat snagged on the wooden decking when he leaped over its side and landed with a soft thud. Their eyes met over the expansive yard before the dark figure whirled about and took off like a shot. Kalabernus had been chasing him now for the past ten minutes.

Recognizing that the figure was beginning to gain distance on him Kalabernus finally skidded to a halt, accepting the inevitable. Paying careful attention to the direction he was going Kalabernus grunted in frustration, his glowing penetrating stare following the man's shape as it grew smaller and smaller.

"Lost him you did," Veranke jeered. Having soared past Kalabernus when he'd come to a stop, the shadowy creature appeared aggravated that he'd halted the hunt.

"Shut it."

"Out of practice, you are," Fallon wheezed, trying to get under his skin.

Kalabernus was annoyed. The 'troublesome three' barely looked winded, though he could see their glowing red eyes narrow to thin slits. Over the years he'd grown to understand this behavior trait. It meant they were becoming enthusiastic about the game and were anxious to see it through.

"Never gonna catch him this way. Need to hunt. Need to gain skill!" Zalman screeched loudly, his oily greenish black form billowed suddenly, becoming a floating mass between him and what lay ahead.

The problem was, they were right.

Taking a moment to catch his breath, he panned the forest for movement. Any animal in the surrounding area had likely been scared away by the sounds of the chase. Standing still and quiet he closed his eyes allowing the noises of the forest to permeate his senses completely. Long ago he'd discovered his ability to see and hear the shadows had somehow heightened his sense of sound which gave him an advantage over most. Listening intently, he attempted to hear it; the ever so slight echo, barely perceptible by most human ears, which signified another living presence nearby.

A heartbeat.

His next prey.

Kalabernus knew that if he really wanted to catch the stalker then he'd have to practice. He'd have to become the man the shadows had always wanted him to be and had once been for a short time.

At one time he could track his prey, just as the stalker did with Ariana. He'd get close too. So close, the animal wouldn't even know he was there until he was within a few feet of them.

Once, he had gotten so close, he'd been able to reach out and touch the animal's snout, instilling instantaneous fear within it. But to accomplish this, he knew he'd have to let them in.

Take over even.

It meant relinquishing his will to the shadows, which he'd promised his father he'd never do again. But this time, things were different. The hunt wasn't a game anymore. It was a means to an end to Ariana's torment. She didn't deserve to be tortured. He on the other hand...

Slowing his breathing, Kalabernus tensed.

Thuh, thuh, *Thuh*. Thuh, thuh, *Thuh*.

There it was.

The sound he'd been seeking.

Crouching low, he stood poised for flight, taking a second to gain his bearing. Shifting his head without even opening his eyes he allowed his own breathing to become still as death.

His head jerked unexpectedly to the south and he was off. Feet cradled within the soft doeskin moccasins he fashioned himself years before, he tread cautiously toward his unwitting quarry. The shadows followed, hovering above and around him. He could tell they were giddy with excitement. Their shapeless forms slipped through the air above and around him as a snake might upon the ground. Their hapless bodies seemed to tremble in anticipation of what was to come. Unusually silent, they slithered about as he moved with a cautious steady gait toward his prey, watching the forest floor for its prints, for its path.

There were twigs to the right near a tree, broken from an animal moving past. A tiny tuft of hair was ensnared upon the small branch of a bush in its path.

A wolf.

They were rare in these parts.

Kalabernus lips curled. Though huge in size like a bear, his brothers had always claimed he had the instincts and stealth of a wolf. His smile came slow, his crystal blue eyes gleaming with a haunting light. It was time to see how right they were and how close he could get.

The closer the better.

He knew he hadn't much time to train.

Kalabernus could feel the darkness enshrouding him like a curtain as the shadows slowly enveloped within him the closer he came. That was the problem with this game. It was the reason his father had insisted he stop. To get that close, so close that he could almost touch it, he had to become like one of them; like the shadows which haunted, which taunted.

If he wasn't careful, if he let them take too great a hold on him, then he could lose himself completely to them. And then...

Then he would kill.

Without compunction or a weapon.

And that's what really made him dangerous.

- - -

Three days later Kalabernus loped into the kitchen mid-morning. Unshaven and wearing the same clothes from the day before, he yawned loudly, stretched, then scratched at the back of his neck. The late nights were taking its toll, but he was getting better and the stalker was getting sloppier, becoming more desperate at being hunted. He'd nearly caught him last night, in fact. But the little devil turned out to be a bit more slippery than he'd anticipated.

Plus, he was cheating.

Discovering the traps, the stalker had made for him Monday night, Kalabernus had opted to turn the tables on him and set some of his own. Unfortunately, this monster of Ariana's was familiar with a fisherman's knot and managed to escape before he could reach him. Kalabernus had clearly spooked him, though, because he'd left behind his night vision glasses.

Pouring himself a mug of coffee he noted the pot was still set on warm. Blinking he shifted his gaze around the kitchen, catching sight of his father at the kitchen table with the newspaper.

How'd he miss seeing him coming in?

"Because you get sloppy when you're tired," Bastion said aloud.

One eyebrow rose. "See now, it's statements like that over the years, that helped me figure out you can read minds." Kalabernus lifted the mug of coffee to his lips. It tasted bitter today, which meant Kahner had made the pot. He was always making it too strong and without the cinnamon he liked in it.

Bastion paused mid-sip, peering over his mug at Kalabernus.

"Yeah, I know. Have known for some time actually," Kalabernus continued. "You think I, of all people, wouldn't figure it out?"

Bastion simply grunted. Shaking out the paper he folded it before him and laid it on the table. "I know what you're doing," was all he said.

"Do you, now?"

"It's not hard to figure out. You spend what time during the day she'll let you spend with her, then you pretend to leave. Instead of coming home, you camp out in the woods hunting her stalker until late in the night."

"Hhhmm. I've got him on edge too."

"Knock it off," Bastion thundered, slamming his hand down on the table for effect.

Anticipating the explosion Kalabernus wasn't really startled. If anything, it simply jarred his head where he was getting a headache from lack of sleep.

Kalabernus fixed his father with a lazy stare. "No," he said simply.

"Are you sure she's worth losing your soul over?"

"Was mom?"

"Was your mother what?"

"Worth losing your soul over," Kalabernus said quietly.

Bastion heaved a troubled sigh. Wincing he rubbed his hands through his salt and pepper colored hair. He'd been afraid of this. His son had fallen head over heels for this woman in a very short time and was liable to get hurt as a result.

"I've been hurt before. It wouldn't be the first time."

"Now who's reading minds?" Bastion countered becoming aggravated.

"There's no point in reading a mind when one can simply read a person's face." He yawned.

Swearing Bastion leaned forward against the table. Clasping his hands before him, he stared back over at Kalabernus with a dark scowl.

"Son, I just wish you would tread carefully where this woman is concerned…"

"I'm not stupid, all right?" Kalabernus said sharply, becoming irritable. He thumped his coffee mug on the table loudly, managing to slosh some out over his hand. "I know it can't go anywhere. A woman shouldn't have to endure mine and my shadows presence for a lifetime."

"Then why are you even pursuing this?" Bastion inquired, becoming just as contentious.

"Seriously?" Kalabernus chuckled humorlessly. "This coming from the same man who decked Heaton just six months ago when he grabbed Angela's breasts in front of everyone in Shenanigan's and proclaimed them as being his property. Incidentally, he was drunk at the time."

"Drunk or not, it was in poor taste and all-around bad behavior on Heaton's part. Someone had to put that man in his place. A woman isn't a man's property," Bastion insisted firmly. "And I get it. I do," he said, shaking his hand in the air as he stood. "She's a single woman being stalked by an unknown assailant who's becoming increasingly aggressive in his tactics towards her."

"Increasingly aggressive tactics?" his son's tone was of one in disbelief. "This guy stabbed Ariana's roommate to death simply because she existed near her. He's after her, intent on getting her, and I am not going to let that happen," Kalturek declared heatedly.

"Be her guardian and protector then. By all means. But why do you have to take this so far? You can't let those shadows into your head," Bastion insisted, seeing Kalabernus was becoming increasingly agitated. "What happens if you let them in long enough to get this guy, and she happens to be present at the time. Huh? What are you going to do then?"

"I would never hurt Ariana," Kalabernus hollered indignantly.

Raising his hand to quiet his son Bastion thought carefully before speaking next. "I know you would never intentionally hurt her. But the truth is that you could. So, I ask you again, why do you have to take things so far?" Bastion asked more quietly, trying to keep his son calm. "Is that what you want to happen? For her to see the darkest side of your nature? To hurt her without meaning to, because you no longer have control of your own self?"

Kalabernus tapped on the countertop with the fingertips of one hand. "No rational person does something, knowing full well they might physically hurt someone they love."

"So...?" Bastion prompted, still wanting an answer.

"So, I can't help it all right? I'm in knots here. I don't know how else to help her. This stalker has her freaking out. She didn't seem the type before, but this guy... He's got her all jumpy and hysterical. Terrified even."

"Freaking out." Bastion murmured thoughtfully. "You say jumpy and hysterical?" He found his son's choice of words curious.

"She's scared to death. It's like she's hearing and seeing things that aren't there."

Bastion stared, his expression unreadable. "You know what? Tonight's Wednesday. Why not invite Ariana to the house for dinner?" he suggested unexpectedly.

"What?" Kalabernus turned back toward him in surprise. This was an unexpected turn of events.

"Invite her over," his father insisted with a shrug. "Why not? Everyone has been coming home on Wednesday evenings lately. Your sisters seem to have taken a real liking to Sable and her kids."

"Yeah, I've noticed," he groaned. "Do you really think that's wise? Bringing her back here, that is? Around everyone?" Kalabernus couldn't help but think it odd his father had changed the subject so abruptly.

"No wiser than you chasing some stalker through the forest at night. But hey, you're gonna do what you're gonna do and because you're an adult and your own man now, I can't stop you. At least this way you get Ariana out of that cabin for a while in a protective environment. It'll give her a chance to unwind and meet some new people. She is new to Loveland, after all."

"Why do I get the feeling you have some ulterior motive with this invite?" Kalabernus asked cautiously.

"Probably because you know me so well," Bastion responded in kind, with a slight grin. He leaned back in his chair, resting one of his booted feet on the opposite leg.

Kalabernus eyed his father suspiciously. After a moment he nodded slowly. "All right. I'll invite her to the ranch but I'm not making any promises."

"Of course, not. That would imply you could keep one," Bastion stated bitterly, his gaze narrowing on his son with an accusatory glare as he got up and stalked away. "Just do me a favor will you?" he called as he paused before disappearing.

"What's that?"

"Don't make me have to shoot you in order to save her," he said caustically.

"Dad," he hollered back, causing him to stop and look back. "Would you? Shoot me that is…to save her?" He fidgeted, anxious to know the truth.

Bastion hesitated briefly then spoke, his voice charged with emotion. "Yes."

Kalabernus stared.

"Good."

Chapter 12

The invitation had been awkward.

Ariana had asked what the occasion was and Kalabernus really didn't have a good answer ready. Stumbling over his words he'd felt like a bumbling idiot and had been relieved when she finally smiled and let him off the hook.

"I'm just teasing you, Kalabernus," she'd said.

He liked the way she said his name.

Then she'd argued with him, stating it was unsafe for her to associate with his family because of the stalker. One of his brothers or sisters could become a target just as he had, she'd pointed out. The whole time he couldn't help but get the feeling she was trying to avoid attending for other reasons. She didn't seem quite herself and was constantly fidgeting, her eyes darting about as if afraid her stalker was about to jump out at her at any moment.

"It's okay," he said finally, giving her the out she was clearly looking for. "I get it, I do. I won't push you to spend time with me outside of your house. I wouldn't want to embarrass you by being seen with me."

"That has nothing to do with it at all. Why in the world would I be embarrassed to be seen with you?" Ariana was astounded by his ridiculous assessment.

"It's okay. Really. Most people are. I'm sure the last thing you want to do, would be to meet any more of my family. I wouldn't want to give them the wrong impression or anything. You know, like we're dating or something." Looking wounded he turned to leave, only to be stopped by her hand on his shoulder.

"Aren't we?" she asked.

"Aren't we what?"

"Dating. I know we've sort of started a bit backward here but... Whether advisable or not under the circumstances, it sure seems like we're seeing each other a lot lately. Don't you think?"

Kalabernus's heart did a little dance in his chest. "Does that mean... Are you my girlfriend then?" he asked abruptly, beginning to sweat at the startled look she gave him. But then she grinned.

He was so sweet, and inexperienced where women and dating were concerned, which was refreshing for Ariana. So often she'd be harangued and harassed by polished men with their silver tongues and it was tiresome to have to fend them off. But with Kalabernus it was different. He never took anything for granted, even the time he spent with her. He seemed to cherish it, as though ever expectant it might be his last.

Reaching up, she pulled him down toward her and deliberately kissed him. She could feel his arms surround her, his hands splaying across her back as he pulled her into a closer embrace.

"Yes."

Kalabernus looked at her intently. He appeared confused. "Wait, yes to dinner at the ranch, or yes to being my – you know – girlfriend."

Ariana giggled. "Yes, to both," she said, smiling brightly. He looked so hopeful and yet stunned at the same time.

Wanting to believe her and anxious to get her out of the cabin and back to his father's horse ranch Kalabernus threw caution to the wind.

He knew it wouldn't last.

Knew it couldn't last.

But for at least a short time he wanted to enjoy the moment. He never had a woman want to be his girlfriend before. Then again, she didn't really know who he was yet.

With not but a little bit of guilt twisting in his gut, he gave a big toothy smile and took her hand in his. Together, they made sure the cabin was locked up and then he walked her to his truck, gallantly assisting her into the vehicle – albeit a bit awkwardly.

Getting into the driver's side he buckled up and started the engine. "I have to warn you, my family, they're a bit different than most." He was nervous, but his excitement was clear in his tone and mannerism.

Ariana became increasingly agitated as they drove along. Sensing her anxiety, he turned toward her and frowned. "Don't worry. They won't hurt you or anything. They might embarrass you, though. But probably not."

Holding tightly to the handhold on the door Ariana watched guardedly as a shadow crept toward her from the backseat. Clasping her hand tightly around the treasure in her pocket she willed the dark creature away, hoping she hadn't just made a bad decision in agreeing to have dinner with his family. The shadowy beings she had been seeing since Saturday night didn't seem to bother her too much if she kept a careful hold of the item in her coat pocket. Their incessant presence was discomforting, nonetheless, and often put her on edge. She truly believed she was going mad.

The drive to the RavenCroft horse ranch was shorter than she'd anticipated, but she was almost grateful for that. An uncomfortable silence had permeated the vehicle until they arrived, mostly from the anxiety they were both experiencing for different reasons.

Ariana marveled over the expansive grounds and beautiful log style ranch house as he pulled up the drive. Set in a very picturesque location one could see the mountains looming in the distance even from the driveway. About fifty yards away she could see a series of horse barns and corrals in addition to a bunkhouse of which made up the extent of the horse ranch.

Pulling up to the house, Kalabernus parked near the walkway. From the looks of all the vehicles in the driveway near the garage, it appeared everyone was already there. Getting out quickly, he rushed around the vehicle, nearly tripping on his feet to open her door for her. Taking her hand, he helped her out and walked her to the door.

Inside, the RavenCroft siblings and their spouses had congregated between the living room and kitchen. Most were catching up on what they'd missed in each other's lives since the last time they'd met the previous week.

"Listen up," Bastion called suddenly from his perch near the fireplace. Gaining everyone's attention he continued quickly, anticipating his son's imminent arrival. "I expect you all on your best behavior tonight."

"Why is tonight any different than any other night?" Drayke asked suspiciously.

"Because tonight we will be having a guest," Bastion said in answer.

The door in the entrance opened before anyone could reply or query. Kalabernus stepped into the house, guiding Ariana along with him.

Synedra turned around in her chair, surprised to see her brother with a woman in tow. Recognizing the woman arriving with Kalabernus as the same one she'd run into at the coffee house, she got up and extended her hand as they came further into the living room.

"Hi there," she greeted her.

"Hello there right back." Ariana took her hand and shook it, smiling brightly. Her eyes shifted hesitantly about the room. "Small world. I tried the mint tea you suggested, by the way. You were right. It was quite helpful and tasted good too."

"You recommended mint tea?" Dr. S.T. Funnie inquired with a raised brow. He'd just come in from the kitchen where he'd been helping to set the tables for his wife Mackenzie. He thought his sister-in-law's advice a bit odd as he knew typically why she would recommend it. Taking one look at Kalabernus's new friend, however, he let out a low whistle and became distracted. The woman was very pleasing to look at. Peering around the room he suspected he'd missed something which irritated him. It seemed like lately, he was always coming in on the tail end of a family drama and Dr. S.T. Funnie sure hated missing the good stuff.

"It seemed fitting at the time," Synedra said in a small voice while glancing between Ariana and her brother, trying to figure out what was going on. He was beaming from ear-to-ear and looked positively stoked for having brought a woman home.

"For those who haven't met her yet, this is Ariana Davis." Kalabernus guided her forward gently with his hand at the small of her back. "She's my girlfriend," he announced proudly.

Bastion's head jerked around suddenly, and he stood. His eyes narrowed upon his son and the woman next to him, who blushed profusely. He shook his head toward Kalturek and Drayke who, nearly choking on their beers, halted their exclamations of surprise abruptly. Greeting Ariana warmly, Bastion welcomed her to his home.

"Thank you. Your invitation was very kind. It's actually kind of nice getting out of the cabin for a bit," Ariana said. "I work from home, you see."

"What do you do that allows you to work from home?" Laynie asked curiously. Her shoulder-length chestnut curls hid her eyes slightly, allowing her to get a good look at Ariana without the appearance of staring.

"I'm a freelance writer."

"You mean like instruction manuals and such? I've heard about people doing that," said a short woman with medium length golden blonde hair standing almost possessively near Kalturek. Ariana presumed she was the Sheriff's wife.

"Some freelance writers handle that sort of thing, but not me. I handle business and technical writing that most companies don't want to, or don't have time to, mess with. You'd be surprised how many companies, and even individuals for that matter, will pass on such odd jobs."

"Sounds lucrative."

"I haven't needed to dip into my parent's inheritance money for years so, yeah, I guess I do okay," she replied, shrugging out of her jacket. Taking it for her, Kalabernus hung it up in the closet then quickly returned to her side.

"Are we eating or what?" Nathan called from the kitchen. Popping his head around the dividing wall he waived at Ariana in greeting. His smile waned briefly, and he shifted his gaze away quickly toward his wife Synedra. They seemed to share a mutually unspoken thought.

"Come on everyone. We don't want to keep Nathan waiting," Bastion said wryly, finding the exchange between his daughter and son-in-law interesting. Something was up.

The family converged upon the kitchen. Taking up plates from the table they headed to the long counter where a makeshift buffet had been set up. Ariana had been relieved to see roasted chicken in the pans with long grain wild rice, and French style green beans.

"Do you all do this, every Wednesday?" she wondered aloud as she dished food onto her plate then glanced around. Kalabernus had said there were six kids in his immediate family but when the spouses were added along with Sable and Kahner's three children, she realized it made for a large crowd.

"We didn't use to," Mackenzie acknowledged. She handed the basket of bread toward Ariana to offer a roll. "But it *has* sort of become a regular Wednesday night deal here lately."

Choosing a roll from the basket Ariana thanked her then moved awkwardly towards the table, unsure of where to sit. Making the decision for her, Kalabernus reached around her and slid out a chair so she could sit. Then he sat down beside her on her right. Ariana noticed Synedra pull out the vacant chair to her left.

"You don't have a drink," Synedra commented while sitting down.

"I guess I forgot to get one." Ariana appeared a bit dazed by the hustle and bustle of the many people in the kitchen. It almost felt like being in a busy restaurant.

Synedra's eyes lit up, thankful for the opportunity which had presented itself. "Kalabernus, why don't you grab her a drink? I'm betting she's not used to finding her way through such a mass of people."

"Right, I'll get it for you." Kalabernus jumped up from his seat, anxious to be helpful and quickly sped away.

Synedra leaned toward Ariana. "Have you told him yet?"

"Told him what?"

"About what's coming," Synedra replied, trying to be tactful.

Perplexed, Ariana gave her a quizzical look. "Sorry. I don't understand what you mean."

Synedra's head tilted and she gave Ariana an appraising stare. Her mouth dropped. "You don't know yet, do you?"

"Know what exactly?" Ariana inquired, baffled by the line of questioning.

Eyes becoming huge, Synedra's head jerked toward Drayke expectantly. "Drayke?" she called. "Is she for real?" she asked, knowing full well he'd been eavesdropping.

Shoulders tense, her brother peered back at his youngest sister. "Far as I can tell. Why?" Drayke asked appearing confused.

From the head of the table, Bastion followed the conversation closely, intent upon learning if his suspicions were correct or not.

That's when it happened.

Exactly what Ariana had feared would happen when she'd accepted the invitation to dinner.

She heard them before she saw them, and her head jerked suddenly in their direction. The black vaporous wisps of smoke funneled into the kitchen from the patio leading off it. Chittering and cackling with glee, they soared toward the table where she sat next to Synedra. Her eyes grew wide with fright.

"I got you a tall glass of milk," Kalabernus said eagerly, having just returned to the table. Aware the shadows were seeping into the kitchen, he was desperately trying to ignore them, but his eyes shifted toward the patio anxiously anyways.

"Please, no. Not now," she whimpered softly, wishing she'd never come. They'd think she was crazy, and Kalabernus would think she'd lost her mind.

"Ariana? Are you okay?" Kalabernus asked with concern.

Ariana began to shake. Reaching for her treasure she realized with dread that she no longer had it in her possession. Having placed it in the pocket of her coat before they'd left her house, she had forgotten to transfer it to her jeans pocket.

"My coat."

"Ariana?"

"I *need* my coat," she declared, trying to keep the despair from her voice unsuccessfully.

"Are you cold?" Kalabernus asked becoming more than a little concerned. Aggravated by the shadows sudden and unwanted presence, he knew whenever they were around they tended to bring the temperatures down.

"No, I need what's in it." Jumping out of her chair she nearly tipped it over in her haste to get away from the table.

"I can get it for you," Kalabernus insisted, confused by her behavior as he stood himself. She looked scared again and he didn't like that. He took hold of her arm in order to stop her.

The shadowy creatures converged upon her, and this time, she realized with horror, that there was more than just three of them. Crying out with fright her whole body trembled violently as she fled the kitchen.

"Wait, Ariana!" Kalabernus called, taking off after her.

Bastion's head drooped with distress the moment he saw recognition go off in his daughter Synedra's eyes. She watched the couple flee the kitchen then stared down the length of the table toward him. Her lips pursed in annoyance and she tossed her fork on the table, gaining everyone's attention.

"You knew, didn't you?" Synedra accused heatedly.

"I had my suspicions," Bastion groaned guiltily. "Come, for I suspect neither one understands."

Chapter 13

Following the couple quickly Bastion took off after them, and Synedra hurried to catch up. They could hear Ariana's cries of distress when she couldn't find her coat right away.

"I need it, Kalabernus – my coat. Where did you put it? Where is it, please?" she begged.

"We've barely even eaten yet. Let's pack some food up to take with us at least," Kalabernus said. Confused and distressed by his girlfriend's sudden desire to leave, he tried to take hold of her arm again in order to get her attention.

Shaking his hand off Ariana desperately continued to search through the coats in the closets. She could hear the frightening sound of the shadows getting closer for they were following them into the living room.

"You don't understand. I have to find my coat," she cried desperately, becoming more and more hysterical. They were getting closer. Tears were forming in her eyes and threatening to fall down her cheeks. She could see a shadow slithering ahead of the rest, the sight of which made her skin crawl in revulsion. Its fleshless arms reached out to her as it screeched and howled with gleeful abandon, enjoying the terror it was instilling within her. It lunged toward her and she jerked violently away, falling to the floor near the coat closet.

Alarmed by the scene Ariana was making Drayke, Mackenzie, Kahner, and Kalturek wandered into the living room followed by their spouses. They watched as she flung herself to the floor near the coats. She looked like she was trying to get away from something.

"What the... Oh, no." Kalturek said suddenly in dismay, watching as Ariana plunged into the coat closet, screaming and crying for her coat. His brother Kalabernus stood over her, too stunned by what was happening to react. "Drayke, do you think it's possible?"

Mackenzie turned toward Drayke, a suspicious look on her face at her other brother's words. "What don't I know?" she asked angrily. "Because I can tell you honestly, whatever is happening to that woman right now is terrifying the crap out of her."

Finally, catching sight of her navy-blue wool jacket, Ariana squealed and shoved her hand into its pocket. "I have to get them away. Please make them go away," she whimpered as her hands shook.

"Wait a minute. Ariana, are you seeing them? Are you seeing the shadows?" Kalabernus exclaimed, having suddenly put the pieces together in his head.

More concerned about getting the item in her pocket into her hand Ariana didn't bother answering him. She didn't figure he'd believe her anyway and it never occurred to her that what he was asking implied he could see them too. Crying out in relief upon snatching her hand around the small metallic item, she clutched it desperately toward her chest and began to murmur softly, closing her eyes as she spoke.

A bright flash of light erupted within the room blinding Drayke at its intensity and the unexpected sight of it. He'd seen the warm balls of light before, but never quite so bright.

"Oh, geez! That is painful," he exclaimed while attempting to shelter his eyes. Across the room, he could see Ariana shading her own eyes from the light, as though she could see it too. Gaping openly in shock his gaze shifted to Kalabernus then back at Ariana. "Wait a minute, you can see that?" he called. "Ariana are you seeing a bright light right now?" he demanded to know, startling the entire household.

Ariana sobbed as she huddled on the floor near the closet, her back braced against the wall, preventing her from fleeing further.

"Yes! It's the only thing that keeps them away," Ariana cried desperately.

"Keeps who away? Who is them?" Kalabernus croaked.

"I don't know what they are. They're like…black shadowy demons or something," she answered him miserably, biting all the while at her lip. She knew the instant she said it they'd be locking her up in a nut house.

Mackenzie's hands flew to her face. *"You're pregnant!"* she cried. "You're pregnant with my brother's baby!"

Heart plummeting to his feet Kalabernus gaped openly at the woman crouching on the floor next to him, then over at his sister, horrified by the notion.

"What would possibly make you think I'm pregnant?" Ariana asked, both perplexed and irritated. They acted like what she was seeing was no big deal to them. Her gaze shifted toward Drayke who stood gaping at her. He'd asked if she could see the light. But how had he known it was there? She stared up at Kalabernus, and suddenly realized she wasn't the only one who could see the black cloudy creatures hovering behind the white light either.

"You can see them? Kalabernus, please tell me. Are you seeing what I'm seeing right now?"

"Yes. I've been able to see the shadows for as long as I can remember. But I've never seen them do this before," Kalabernus admitted. "Acting afraid, shrieking in pain, and desperate to get away but unable to."

The light began to fade, and Ariana began mumbling softly, determined to keep the light with her for longer.

Bending down next to her, Kalabernus watched the shadows writhe and swirl about angrily, their jowls and arms bending in an unnatural fashion. Moments later they exploded, like a gigantic ink splash, within the open space of the living room and seeped out through the windows.

Ariana continued to huddle on the floor as she whispered, oblivious to the scene since she'd closed her eyes off from the sight of the frightening creatures. Seeing her shiver Kalabernus awkwardly placed his arms around her.

"How long have you been able to see the shadows?"

Sniffling, Ariana finally looked up at him after snuggling up closer to him for warmth and comfort. "Since Saturday?" she answered tentatively. Her free hand trembled against his arm.

Kalabernus inhaled sharply. "The figure in the patio doorway... You were seeing Veranke."

"Veranke?" Ariana was confused. A tear escaped down her cheek. "You...you don't think I'm crazy?" she stammered, starting to become suspicious. Though she could no longer see or sense the shadows nearby, she couldn't quite seem to stop shaking.

Holding her tighter Kalabernus closed his eyes then shook his head. "I'm so sorry. I had no idea. It's not...not even supposed to be possible," he stammered.

"What's not possible? I don't understand." She looked at him, her appearance mimicking that of a frightened and wounded young girl who was becoming angry.

"You can see them because *I* can see them," Kalabernus admitted finally. "The fact that I can see these demonic shadows is kind of a family secret. It's why everyone is always afraid of me and intimidated by me because they're always around me."

It took a minute before Ariana fully registered what he was saying.

Kalabernus could see the instant understanding dawned on her.

"It's an inherited trait, isn't it? I can only see them now because I'm..." her voice faltered. Her eyes widened, too stunned to continue. She clasped a hand to her abdomen.

"Pregnant," Kalabernus finished for her.

The silence lasted for all of about ten seconds before the explosion hit as both Laynie and Stephanie turned toward their husbands and began shouting in unison, their speech overlapping in places. The abrupt commotion initially startled Ariana.

"Are you kidding me...?"

"-Drayke! What the heck is..."

"-Going on here?"

"-Why can they?"

"What exactly does this mean?" Laynie yelled above Stephanie.

"It means you all need to take this argument elsewhere," Bastion insisted, seeking to temper the fighting for the time being.

"We're taking it elsewhere all right," Laynie declared, huffing from the house without a backward glance or coat.

Stephanie, on the other hand, looked defeated. "Why is it that everyone in this family who wants to get pregnant can't, and those who don't or aren't planning to, can?" she demanded of her husband.

Knuckles against his hips Kalturek sighed in exasperation, tired of hearing the same question over and over again. "We've been through this Stephanie..." Before he could finish, the blonde headed bombshell fled the house, wailing loudly as she ran.

Trembling, Ariana got to her feet, dragging her coat with her. Something else had suddenly connected in her mind as she watched the women storm from the house.

"Let me get this straight, you can see the shadows, Kalabernus, but you cannot see the light that was here?" she asked, then pointed toward Drayke. "But you can see the light. If it's an inherited trait, then does that mean that all of you can see one or the other?"

"No," Kahner responded before his father could. "And, yes, I know we need to tread carefully here Dad, but I think she has the right to know under the circumstances."

Ariana's gaze shifted cautiously from Bastion back to Kahner. Was it possible Kahner was reading his dad's thoughts somehow?

"It's more than a little possible actually," Kahner said aloud, startling her. She gasped audibly, her eyes growing ever wider with shock.

"Let's just slow down here. Learning everything in one night might be too much in her condition," Dr S.T. said, becoming concerned for Ariana's well-being. He looked to his wife for support. "Wouldn't you agree, Mackenzie?"

Head jerking to attention at hearing her name, Mackenzie gave an automatic response. "Yes, of course." She was distracted. Kalabernus had fathered a child barely a month after Kahner had? The two conceptions occurring within such a short time of each other seemed too much of a coincidence. None of them was supposed to be able to have children. What could this possibly mean?

"Everything? Wait...there's more? And why can I see both the shadows and that light thing, but neither of you can?" Ariana gestured between Kalabernus and Drayke. Though somewhat relieved to learn she wasn't going completely crazy, she had begun to think she'd ventured into the twilight zone.

"That's a very good question." Bastion stepped forward and gazed between his two sons then back at Ariana thoughtfully.

"Ariana, what exactly are you holding?" Mackenzie inquired. She was curious about what it was that had Ariana fleeing to her coat at the sight of the shadowy creatures.

"This old thing?" Ariana spoke softly, opening her hand so they could see. Laying in the palm of her hand was a three-inch piece of silver that had been fashioned into the shape of a cross. "It was given to me by my sister, Sareena a year before she died in the car accident."

"It looked like the moment you latched onto it the bright light appeared." Drayke glanced toward the front door becoming anxious at Laynie's absence. He knew he'd need to go after her soon or he'd pay for it later.

Ariana turned toward Kalabernus and explained. Tears were welling in her eyes as she spoke. "Ever since my sister gave it to me I've used it as a bit of a crutch, I guess. Whenever I'd get scared as a child, I'd hold onto it and recite the prayer she taught me. Sunday night the shadows were all over me, and I was hearing terrifying noises outside the cabin as well. So, I pulled it from the box I keep it in and began the prayer. That's when I saw the light for the first time."

Kalabernus's breathing was heavy. His eyes shifted to his father then back at her hand. Reaching toward her extended hand he flinched, hesitant about touching the item, yet somehow compelled to do so.

"Ariana, may I … may I hold it?" Kalabernus asked anxiously.

Uneasy about relinquishing her treasure Ariana paused before responding. "So l…long as I can h…have it back," she stuttered nervously. Their eyes met, both clearly overwhelmed at the notion of her being pregnant.

"Of course."

Hands shaking, Kalabernus took hold of the tiny cross with two fingers. Placing it in the palm of his other hand he gazed around the room as if waiting almost expectantly to see the light that she had.

"I don't … I don't see it," he croaked. "Drayke," he called before his brother disappeared through the front door. "Where was the light when it came? What did it do?"

"I couldn't say for sure what it was doing without being able to see the shadows response but… The light was immediately in front of her when it came. It seemed to radiate out."

"And the shadows exploded, then fled through the window," Kalabernus said in a choked voice, disturbed by what it meant. "Dad, the light … it was protecting her!"

"Sort of acting like a barrier maybe?" Nathan questioned thoughtfully. He and Bastion exchanged looks

"Why doesn't it come for me? Why has it never attempted to protect me?" Kalabernus asked, becoming thoroughly distressed.

"Maybe…maybe because she's pregnant?" Synedra offered, trying to lessen what was obviously beginning to upset her brother. Her heart ached for him. "She wasn't born with it, but her child will be?" she stated with a questioning glance toward her father. Bastion's nod of agreement was slight.

"So, our son will one day be cursed like me? He'll see what I see all the time? Without any barrier of light?" Kalabernus exclaimed in alarm.

"Or daughter," Kalturek offered quietly. Deciding it best he go after his own wife, he glanced back at his brother in concern before disappearing through the door.

Kalabernus let out an excruciating yelp of distress. Agitated, he ran his hands through his short black hair and paced before Ariana, shaking his head.

"No! This can't happen. I won't let it happen. Bring up a child as cursed as I have been? And a little girl at that? Absolutely not. It ends with me. It must end with me."

Chapter 14

Yup, that's right. Ariana might well be in the family way.

I think it safe to say that no one in the RavenCroft family saw this coming except for maybe Bastion RavenCroft. It might even be fair to say that he was tipped off by what his son Kalabernus had been saying about the way she had been acting. Having watched his son being tormented for so long by the 'troublesome three,' he was more than familiar with the little nuances of Kalabernus's response to them. And though it had been over forty years, he still had prevalent memories of how his late wife Inara had acted when she'd been pregnant with his sons. So, knowing that at one point they'd been intimate and hearing Kalabernus describe Ariana's behavior as "freaking out," and "jumpy," in addition to "hysterical" the pieces just started falling into place.

Bastion's suspicions weren't fully realized, though, until he saw how Ariana acted in the kitchen and witnessed his youngest daughter Synedra's knowing gaze. For Synedra had the ability to know when a woman was with child. What was interesting to him was that Ariana appeared to be seeing the light that his son Drayke could see. When their mother Inara had been pregnant with the three boys she had also seen the same bright white balls of light. She had not seen them, however, when she got pregnant the second time around with Drayke and Mackenzie. This had him wondering if Ariana was seeing the light simply because it was protecting her, or if there was another reason entirely.

For obvious reasons Ariana was now feeling extremely overwhelmed by everything that was happening and what she was learning.

Shoot, wouldn't you if you were in her shoes?

As if being stalked by a nutcase who murdered her roommate wasn't enough, now she's…

…receiving the dreaded threats once again, she's…

…been drugged by said stalker who had heaven only knows what intent for her that night, she…

…wound up sleeping with a man she didn't really know as a result, she's…

…now seeing creepy and frightening black shadowy creatures, she's…

…also seeing warm bright balls of light, she's…

…finding out she's pregnant and that this is the reason for her newfound "abilities," and she's…

…also discovering that not only is she not the only one who could see them but that there are others within the RavenCroft family who are capable of extraordinary abilities.

Ariana was very confused about her situation and more than a little embarrassed that Kalabernus's entire family was now fully aware of what had transpired between them. His response to learning the news had upset her a great deal also for she didn't believe in ending a life at any stage. So, she didn't know quite what to make of him. Did he truly believe that giving life was truly an option?

As you can probably imagine, at that moment she felt desperate, trapped, and just wanted to escape their knowing eyes. She needed time to think but he had driven her there. She had no way home. So, Ariana did the only thing any self-respecting woman in her shoes would do.

She demanded the keys to Kalabernus's truck.

- - -

"What have I done? I've cursed Ariana. I've cursed my own child," Kalabernus exclaimed.

After demanding the keys to his vehicle, Ariana fled the RavenCroft ranch house. He could hear the engine of his truck turn over and the squeal of his tires as she tore out of the drive. The way her face had screwed up in anguish over what she'd learned and what he'd said haunted him.

He was a monster.

He didn't deserve her.

"Stop it. That's enough," Bastion demanded, becoming cross at his son's thoughts.

"Who could possibly want this? Who could love a monster? A devil? She should abort it; she needs to abort it. I cannot ask her to carry this burden."

"You were never a burden to either your mother or me," Bastion insisted angrily, upset that his son felt taking a child's life was even an option.

"Wasn't I? I remember the stories mama would tell of when she carried me, and she'd see them, and…"

"She told you those stories to help you understand you weren't alone. To help you see that she knew first-hand what you were going through. I would posit to say it's likely one of the reasons, a mother pregnant with a child meant to be gifted, experiences what she does. So she can help them learn to understand their ability as they grow up. She loved you with all her heart. She…*we*…" Bastion insisted forcefully, "-Wanted you. You were always wanted by me and your mother. And you have always been loved by us both. Even on up to the day she died."

Kalabernus snorted in disgust and gave his father a disbelieving look as he began to pace.

Bastion fumed. "Are you telling me you could never love your own son or daughter if they were to be born with the ability to see and hear the shadows?

"I never said that," Kalabernus snapped.

"Then what is your issue?"

"Because I know, all right! I know what it's like to live with this day in and day out. The demons ever-present all around, heckling me, taunting me, convincing me to do things sometimes that I don't even want or mean to do."

"So, don't do it."

Kalabernus scoffed again. "That's easier said than done. You have no idea. For a child to be born with this again…" He shook his head in denial. "No, it needs to end. It must end with me."

"Who's to say it might not be different for your child?" Drayke interjected, coming back into the house with Kalturek. His wife was nowhere to be seen. She'd apparently taken off with his brother's wife Stephanie for his car was missing.

Bastion gave Drayke a calculating look. "What do you mean?"

Drayke pointed in the direction of the front door where Ariana had escaped moments before. "What if Kalabernus was always meant to see both? Because she's seeing both. Ariana said it herself just before she left. Sometimes it's a greenish-black inky smoke and other times it's like a cloudlike ball of bright white light – like what I see."

The family exchanged looks, trying to connect the dots Drayke had already managed to string together.

Snapping his fingers, Nathan gestured toward Drayke. "I see what you're getting at. One is meant to offset the other. Like Kalturek being able to see auras. Black and white. Good versus evil intentions."

"Exactly. What if I was never meant to have that ability? Maybe my gift was only ever meant to be, to know when people are lying."

Mackenzie was doubtful. "For all we know, the white light and knowing the truth are linked. Besides, if you weren't meant to have that ability then how did you come by it?"

"I don't know but the light isn't always present when I'm learning a truth. Their appearances are random. That is, except for the one I'm always seeing next to you," Drayke pointed toward Kahner.

"I always have a light next to me?" Kahner swiveled where he stood as though attempting to see what his brother was. "Is it there now?"

"Oh, yeah. I've been able to see its presence near you since we were twelve. It's the same now. There's one near Sable now too," Drayke answered.

"There's a light present near me?" Sable responded in awe.

"Every time I see you, it's there," he insisted with a half-smile. Drayke turned toward his father. "Dad, what if..." his voice trailed off as though deep in thought.

"What is it Drayke?" Bastion prompted.

"I don't know. I just have this gut feeling like something big is happening. I can't explain it. It's as if something is being set in motion here." He fixed his father with a calculating look and knew in that very instant that Bastion too had been experiencing the same sensation, but for much longer than he had.

"What do you know that we don't?" Drayke asked suspiciously, confronting his father.

Bastion just looked at him, his gaze piercing right through him. "I have no idea what you're talking about, Boy." Turning about he walked briskly away.

- - -

The shadows converged on her once again as Ariana attempted to drive back to her cabin. Unable to see through the windshield and frightened that she might have an accident as a result, she pulled over to the side of the road and stopped. Shaking from anxiety she was afraid to attempt driving again once she'd managed to fend them off with her treasure and the light she was seeing.

She locked the doors, making sure the windows were tightly shut. Feeling chilled, she searched the extended cab of the truck for something to help keep her warm. Finding a thick wool blanket Ariana curled up beneath it. Tired from the stress of the evening and having not slept well the past few nights, she soon fell into a fitful sleep.

Ariana's dreams ended up being as bizarre as her reality. She found herself walking at a steady pace along a path at the edge of an expansive field. As she strode along in one direction she dreamed that a very large gray wolf, tinged with blue by the light of the moon, was running in the open field in the opposite direction she'd been walking. Catching sight of her, it veered off course and ran toward her. It's pale, almost crystal blue eyes had a haunting look to them but oddly she felt no fear of the creature running toward her.

Once the wolf came near, it leaped at her, wrapping its legs about her bare arm.

It clung to her.

Bending its head, the wolf clamped its mouth around her arm as though to bite her, but it didn't hurt her or rip at her. She attempted to shake the wolf off, but it refused to release its grasp of her. The wolf's coat was beautiful, and its pale blue eyes were bright with a soft light as they peered up at her from its perch. Under one eye Ariana could see the animal had been wounded for it bled from scratches it had received, and yet, the other eye dripped with a single shining tear of sadness; of heartache and loneliness.

Ariana empathized with the wolf. She felt she could relate to its pain. Reaching out to the wolf with the free hand holding the silver cross, she touched the soft fur at its chest. The wolf howled suddenly with a soulful mournful cry of despair. Though alarmed by the wolf's presence she realized she wasn't afraid of it, for it seemed to have taken a protective hold of her. Sensing she was awakening, as the sound of tapping against glass penetrated her mind, she could feel her heart rate increasing. Her breathing became rapid.

She woke abruptly, blinking several times to clear her vision. Anxiety surged within her at the sight of a figure through the fogged-up window looking in at her as it tapped on her window. Her first impression was of a dark shadow, like the demons who had been haunting her.

Squeezing her eyes shut, afraid her tormentors had returned, she reached for the treasure in her pocket. Strengthened by the feel of the metal piece in her hand, she opened her eyes cautiously. She peered through the haze, confused and yet relieved to realize what she was seeing was the wolf from her dream, tinged by the soft blue light of the moon. There were no scratches or blood but there was a single sad tear trickling down its cheek. Sitting up she leaned toward the door to get a closer look, anxious to reach out and comfort the wolf in his sadness.

- - -

Agitated and unable to eat as a result Kalabernus paced the living room floor while those who were still present ate dinner then dispersed to their own homes. Ariana had been gone for only a couple hours, but her absence was already feeling like it had left a hole inside him. Worried about how upset she had been when she left in his truck Kalabernus borrowed one of his father's vehicles and took off toward her cabin.

Learning that she was pregnant had him all twisted up inside. He was even more intent on locating and catching her stalker, so he'd driven toward the cabin, intending to park on the outskirts and begin his search. Observing as he drove that the shadows had been curiously absent from his presence, he worried over it.

Not paying attention to the road and his surroundings he nearly missed seeing his truck off on the side of the road as he came upon it. A jolt of fear took hold of his senses, bringing him out of his daze from the past couple of hours. He quickly exited his vehicle and strode toward the truck, the darkness enshrouding him as he walked. The sun had set some time ago and the moon was high in the sky.

Anxious at what he might find, he peered cautiously through the fogging driver's side window. Kalabernus could see her sleeping fitfully. He tried the door handle and realized it was locked but he didn't have his spare key. Afraid he might scare her if he woke her, he rested his forehead against the windowpane and sadly watched her sleep. The ache inside that he'd long ago managed to hide swelled within him.

He wished he were a different man.

A normal man.

The kind of man she deserved and needed.

He wondered, not for the first time, at why he'd been cursed to see what he could. It occurred to him then, that even if he managed to catch her stalker, she would simply be trading one demon for another.

Gazing longingly at the woman sleeping in his truck, his thoughts shifted as his eyes roamed over her. He could see her chest lift and fall repetitively as she slept fitfully.

A baby.

He'd always wanted a child.

Like his brothers and sisters, he'd dreamed of one day having them. Kalabernus had always known, in his case, it could never happen; should never happen.

How could he ask this of her?

How could he possibly hope she'd want to carry his child to term; to endure the torment as he did?

And then to raise a child in such a cursed state...

He wept openly as a silent tear threatened to trickle down his cheek. Noticing she was waking he was too miserable to even bother wiping away his tears. She sat up and leaned toward him. The way she looked at him made him feel as though she were seeing him for who he truly was for the first time. They stared at each other intently.

After a moment he heard the click of the lock being released and she opened the door. Unable to control himself any longer Kalabernus sobbed where he stood.

"I'm so sorry, Ariana. The last thing I ever wanted was to hurt you," he wailed painfully, his voice rising in distress as he spoke. The sound of his voice was unnatural even to his own ears.

Ariana reached out and encircled him with her arms. He stiffened.

"How can you do that? How can you want to hold me – want to be near me – after what I've done to you?"

She shushed him, all the while bravely biting her lip, taking strength from the treasure within her grasp. What would her sister do, she thought?

"It's okay Kalabernus…"

"No," he exclaimed with a strangled cry. "No, it's really not. Who wants to be burdened with this? I ask you, who could possibly ever love a child like that?"

"Or do you mean you?" she asked softly, her knowing eyes giving way to the truth of his greatest fear.

Kalabernus stared at her, the pain too excruciating to bear. His heart ached even more.

"Let me ask you something. Your mother and father; did they love each other?"

He laughed bitterly. "I can only dream of such a love as that. It about broke my father when she died."

"Don't you see? That heart beating within your chest was formed out of love. The love between your mother and father. Regardless of whether you can see and hear the shadows that won't ever change. Your heart doesn't belong to those vile creatures any more so than mine does to the man who stalks me."

"What...what does this mean? What are you...?"

"It means we'll figure this out *together*. Help me to figure this out. Don't leave me alone in this."

Kalabernus appeared confused. "I don't... What are you saying? You actually want to try and carry this child?"

Ariana whimpered softly, unsure initially how to respond.

Tired of standing at the side of his truck Kalabernus crawled in next to her and closed the door. Ariana scooted over in the seat to give him room. Surprising him, she immediately leaned back into him for warmth and comfort once he'd situated. Turning on the vehicle, he started the heater.

"I won't lie to you," she began. "I *am* scared."

He gently wrapped his huge hands around her head in an attempt to console her and began running his thick fingers through her soft hair. "I'm sorry," he croaked on a sob. "After everything you've been through, you shouldn't have to deal with this. You deserve better. You deserve to be free of the darkness I live in."

Ariana became thoughtful. "One thing I learned early on from my sister before she died, is that there is a reason for everything that happens, however small or minor it might seem at the time. Stuff we live through and experience is meant to help prepare us for the future to come."

"You can't honestly believe that fate meant for you to suffer through being tortured by a stalker," he said disdainfully. "What? Just to prepare you for becoming pregnant with a child who will one day see shadows?"

"Who better to endure such fear than one who's already lived in fear. Besides, I have a light which seems to protect me." Ariana pointed out the windshield in the direction she'd been heading. "It happened again, as I was heading home. It's why I pulled over. Clearly, it is not the same as it is with you."

"No, you're right. I've never had that." Kalabernus sulked, unable to prevent himself from wallowing in self-pity. "But I am ever so grateful that it comes for you," he earnestly continued, shifting so he could look down at her.

Ariana lifted her head toward him, becoming serious as she spoke. "My sister also taught me that life is precious, and it shouldn't be taken for granted. If I am pregnant as you and your family seem to believe..."

"You are most certainly with child. How else would this be possible otherwise?"

Ariana was silent.

Kalabernus breathed deeply, his eyes wet with unshed tears. His head hurt from lack of sleep and he simply couldn't think straight anymore.

"Our powers are inherited from my father's side of the family," he offered up, trying to help her understand.

"Your father? Does that mean he is gifted too?" Ariana asked.

He nodded. "Yes, he knows things he shouldn't without knowing why or how. According to my late grandmother Sapphire it's a gift she called 'Knowing.'"

"I see."

"He also sees future events, and like my brother Kahner, he has the ability to read minds. Ah, but don't say anything about that last power to the rest of the family. The fact he can read minds isn't widely known by everyone else." He winced at his blunder. "I sort of figured it out by accident."

"Of course, mum's the word." She ran her fingers across her lips then pretended to turn an imaginary key and throw it away. "Anything else I should know?" Ariana asked, wondering why Bastion RavenCroft was withholding the fact he had the ability to know a person's thoughts from the rest of his family.

Kalabernus groaned. "There's so much to tell you. I don't even know where to begin."

"Begin with the beginning."

"In order to do that, we will need to return to my father's house."

"Why?" she asked curiously, unsure whether she wanted to be around his family after the spectacle she made of herself.

"Because there is a book there that you will need to see. It will help you understand as I tell you everything. Sort of a family tree."

"All right. Then take me home."

Adjusting in his seat Kalabernus put the vehicle in gear, continuing forward in the direction of the cabin. The thought of hunting the stalker was far from his mind for the moment.

Ariana tapped him on the shoulder. "Kalabernus, where are you going?"

"Going? Oh, right. Dad's ranch." He grinned at her sheepishly. "Feels like I should be taking you back to our cabin," he admitted while turning the vehicle around.

"Our cabin?" she queried with a raised brow.

His face colored in embarrassment. "What I meant to say…"

She giggled unexpectedly. "It's okay. I feel the same way."

Chapter 15

The next morning Bastion found his new daughter-in-law, Sable, reading in the kitchen when he came down to breakfast. The relative quiet of the kitchen surprised him. Usually, his grandchildren were sitting with her eating breakfast.

"Kahner took their breakfast up to them this morning," Sable said from behind her book. "You know, because of our guest sleeping in the other room?"

Bastion noted Sable sounded slightly perturbed. Having seen Kalabernus and Ariana return to the house the night before, Bastion knew they were curled up in the living room together where they fell asleep. The couple had been up talking much of the night.

Crossing the room to the coffee pot he caught sight of her book cover and paused briefly in surprise. "Find something interesting to read, did we?"

Sable peered over her book "Hhhmm? Yes, it's really quite fascinating."

"Oh? Why's that? What's it about?"

"A family with paranormal powers," she laughed. "Seems almost ironic considering."

Bastion harrumphed softly. "Ironic, right. Is the story any good?"

"Actually, it's quite good. This David Pearson guy could almost be writing about this family if I didn't know better."

"Where'd you find that anyway?"

"What? The book?" Sable inquired, thinking his interest odd. "I've had it since before I came here – brought it with me. I understand it's part of a series. Mackenzie saw me reading it the other night and asked to borrow it. So, I'm trying to finish it."

Eyes twinkling Bastion grabbed a mug and poured himself a cup of coffee. "Did she? How did you say you came by that book again?"

"I didn't actually," Sable replied with a frown. Her head shifted slightly, and she eyed him from behind her book while taking a bite of her scrambled eggs. Distracted by something she thought she'd heard in the living room, both their heads jerked in that direction.

Bastion scowled. "I swear it's like I'm still surrounded by a bunch of juveniles," he vented, his gaze piercing through the screen. He knew exactly what was about to happen.

Sable chuckled, her book forgotten for the moment.

"You want I cover for you?" she inquired, getting up from her chair. Rubbing her hands together, she moved toward the door connecting into the living room.

"Yes, please." Bastion hung his head as he shook it. "And you wondered why I kept my ability to read minds from them."

Sable just smiled in good humor and winked. Stepping through the door she stretched her arm out and whispered loudly to the figure hovering over the couple sleeping on the couch.

"Don't. You. Dare."

Kahner looked back at her with a guilty expression. Poised ready to drop a giant red water balloon on his brother's head, he halted mid-throw.

"Oh, come on," Kahner whispered back. Lifting his arms into a shrug, he allowed the balloon to droop over the back of his hand. "I'll never get a chance like this again."

"You got that right," came a growl from the couch. Rolling Ariana to the floor as she giggled, Kalabernus raised up without warning and slammed Kalturek's hand holding the balloon against his own chest.

"Awe, man," Kahner exclaimed as a large watermark spread down the front of his shirt when the balloon burst. Water dripped from his hands and arms as well as down his jeans.

Ariana wrinkled her nose up at Sable in appreciation as she smiled. "Thanks."

"Don't mention it. I figure we ladies have to stick together in this house." Catching sight of something through the front window that was sitting on the patio she tilted her head curiously. "I wonder what that is?"

Everyone turned to look in the direction she was.

"What's what?" Kahner asked, moving to the end of the couch to get a better view, he spotted what his wife was looking at. "That's odd. It's too early for deliveries."

Striding toward the front door he opened it and brought the parcel in from outside. "It looks like it's for you Kalabernus." He handed it off to his brother.

"I didn't order anything."

Taking the box from his brother he made quick work of breaking the tape then opened the flaps.

"*Stop!*" Bastion shouted suddenly from the kitchen doorway. He'd gotten the image of his son opening the package too late. A split-second later Ariana was screaming and Kalabernus could be heard roaring with rage.

Lifting from within the box a life-size baby doll he flung it across the room. The chest cavity of the doll had been ripped open and the guts of a small cat or dog had been placed within it. Blood oozed from the doll and dripped to the floor. Kalabernus's hands, covered in the blood, shook as he stared at them, his face registering a visceral desire to pulverize the sender.

Kalabernus was unsure when exactly his feelings had changed about the impending baby. Maybe it had been last night, standing outside of his truck as he'd watched Ariana sleep curled up in its seat. Or maybe it had been during the night as he told Ariana of his family and about the supernatural abilities his siblings had been born with. But one thing he knew for certain, he wanted the baby Ariana carried just as much as he wanted the woman who carried it. He'd be damned before he'd allow anyone to harm either one. The stalker had gone too far.

He raged, pacing the living room as Ariana huddled on the floor near the couch. Hands fisted over her mouth as she rocked in place, she stared in horror at the baby doll lying on the floor across the room.

"I don't...I don't understand," she wailed in dismay. Confusion and fear contorted her porcelain features into an anguished mess. "How does he know?" she cried, her gaze jerking toward the giant of a man who abruptly stopped pacing. "How can he possibly know? We just found out last night. *I* just found out we're having a baby last night. I haven't even had the chance to tell Angela yet."

"The only two places you've been since we learned you were expecting was here and..."

"In my truck," Kalabernus finished for Kahner.

Sable's head jerked toward Bastion. The same thought running through both their heads was now running through Kahner's.

"The truck is bugged," Kahner said quietly, voicing that which everyone was thinking.

"And or the house," Sable offered, gaining Bastion's attention.

Lifting his hand to his mouth Bastion placed a finger across his lips, shushing everyone by shaking his head silently. Then turning toward Kahner, using sign language, he informed him that everyone should stay put until his return. He was about to head down the hallway when he noticed the leather-bound book lying on the coffee table. Snapping his fingers to gain Kalabernus's attention he gestured toward him, the book, and Ariana with a questioning look.

Face lighting with understanding Kalabernus groaned aloud as Kahner exhaled sharply. He'd told Ariana everything last night. About how his father had been spirited away at the age of three by his mother Sapphire Blackthorne and brought to Colorado to be adopted and raised by the RavenCroft family. Wanting, to be honest, and open with her about everything, he'd even told her about how Bastion had visited Montana after his birth mother had died and discovered that his identical twin brothers, Rafe and Rourke, had quarreled over a woman who had been impregnated and nearly killed by Rourke. The story had been important to share because within each set of triplets in the Blackthorne line it seemed was one with a dark nature and he'd needed her to know what she was getting into.

Inhaling deeply Kalabernus ran his hands across his face in agitation. He'd even gone into detail about what each family member's abilities were, how they used them, and how some could be tripped up by people. If Ariana's stalker had been listening in somehow, then he now knew everything and that posed a danger to the entire RavenCroft family.

For the next several minutes the three men signed back and forth across the room. The women watched in fascination. Neither were aware the men knew sign language, so the silent conversation had come as a shock to them both.

"What exactly did you tell her?" Bastion asked with his hands.

"Everything," Kalabernus responded just as silently.

"Everything. Meaning what exactly?" Kahner signed, looking furious.

"Everything, meaning everything," Kalabernus responded with silent hands, looking just as peeved.

Bastion growled deep in his throat, shaking his fisted hands in the air while glaring at his son. "What were you thinking?" he asked, contorting his fingers as needed to pose the question.

"I was thinking she is pregnant with my child and needs to know what she is getting into when we get married," Kalabernus responded with silent hands.

"Married? Are you daft? You just met her!" Kahner signed across the room to his brother, his face showing signs of incredulity.

"And how long did you know Sable before you got her pregnant and married her?" Bastion countered, twisting his hands and fingers about. He gestured toward Sable causing her to step back in alarm.

"Wait, how did I get into this?" Sable said aloud.

All three men waved their hands toward her in frustration. Their gesticulating arms stopped abruptly as each one attempted to try and sign to the other. Becoming disgusted, Bastion grunted angrily. Throwing his arms out in frustration he swung around and disappeared down the hall.

"Be back. Stay put. Shut up," Bastion thought harshly, knowing Kahner would tell his brother. The rude gesture Kalabernus flung Kahner's way was proof he'd passed less than half the message on.

Several minutes went by before Bastion returned carrying a duffel bag in hand. Pulling out a small black box with a knob on the top he twisted the knob and set it on the coffee table. Then, retrieving several smaller black items, looking a lot like remote controls only with fewer buttons and a gauge, he began tossing one each to his sons.

"Since when do you keep audio jammers and multifunctional counter surveillance GPS bug detectors on hand?" Kahner asked aloud, stunned by his father's bag of cool toys.

"This is a bug detector?" Kalabernus inquired, looking more than just a little disappointed. He peered down at the small rectangular plastic item in his hand.

"What did you expect? A long stick perhaps?" Bastion asked irritably.

Kalabernus made a face and shrugged self-consciously. "Maybe." His response had a defiant tone.

"You never answered my question," Kahner accused, eyes narrowing.

"Didn't I?" Bastion asked innocently. Strolling around the room he disregarded his son's expressions of annoyance, concentrating instead on locating the offending bugs in question.

"Are these the ones not affected by the audio jammer?" Kahner asked, investigating his device fully.

"What do you think?" Bastion answered almost irately.

"Looks like it has a white noise generator on it," Kahner commented. "The audio jammer is sort of overkill really."

"Kahner, just go check his truck, will you? We'll deal with it in here," Bastion said, his exasperation showing he was losing his patience.

Noticing Ariana was still staring in distress at the bloody doll on the floor Sable grabbed up the box and crossed the room. Picking up the offending doll she placed it back in the box and closed the lid.

"We'll bury it later. For now…"

"Just dump it in the kitchen trash, Sable. It's going out today anyway," Bastion told her. He continued around the room slowly, moving the box in his hand near objects as he came close to them. Frowning, as he watched the gauge on the box, he glanced toward Ariana still cowering near the couch. Appearing thoughtful he walked toward her. The read-out began to spike silently the closer he came to her.

"I need you to stand up please, Ariana," Bastion said, gaining Kalabernus's attention.

"Me? Why?" she asked in surprise.

"Please, just humor an old man."

Pushing up from the floor she used the seat cushions of the couch to help herself up the rest of the way. Adjusting her shirt awkwardly she gazed over at Kalabernus anxiously.

Bastion waived the box slowly from head to foot. The closer he came to the floor the higher the reading. Twisting his head about, his angled view of the floor allowed him to see the purse that had wedged itself beneath the couch near her feet. With grim satisfaction he snatched up her purse, setting it on the coffee table. The reading spiked once again when he ran it over the opening of her purse.

Quirking an eyebrow at her, Bastion inquired. "Permission to rifle through your purse?"

"By all means."

Within seconds they'd discovered a listening device expertly hidden within the little box she kept her tiny cross in.

Ariana's face blanched. Somehow the stalker had known she carried it everywhere with her and had managed to get in her house in order to plant the bug in the box.

"He must have heard everything we said. Everything we did."

Kalabernus and Ariana locked gazes with each other. Not only had the stalker listened in on private moments and conversations between them but he was now aware of the RavenCroft family's secrets. An outsider knew about his entire family and what they could do.

His jaw clenching, a guttural animalistic growl emitted from deep within Kalabernus's chest and throat. Eyes flashing with barely concealed rage he made his decision. Bending down he enclosed Ariana about the back of her neck with his hand and gently brought her towards him. Devouring her lips within a fierce kiss he then released her unexpectedly. Whirling around he stormed toward the entryway and stairwell.

"Where do you think you're going?" Bastion hollered after him, concerned by the determined look in his son's eye.

Kalabernus paused briefly then continued up the stairs without looking back. "Hunting."

"Should I be worried?" Ariana quietly asked the room at large while staring after him. His kiss had been so intense it had shaken her to her core.

"No," Bastion responded in a clipped tone.

"Yes," Kahner said at the same time.

The men locked gazes, their expressions giving the impression a silent war was waging between them.

"Yes," Kahner insisted.

"No," Bastion countered fiercely, thinking all the while, "Don't freak her out dummy."

"She's already freaked out," Kahner argued silently. "And did you just call me a dummy? Really?"

Ariana exchanged a wary glance with Sable.

"Do they do this silent monolog thing often?" she queried aloud.

Sable rolled her eyes. "More often than you might think."

"Huh, wonder if I'm gonna get to read minds, too." Ariana couldn't help but think it might be a slightly advantageous power to have.

"No," Bastion said aloud suddenly. He appeared to be looking at Ariana or was he responding to Kahner?

"That's funny because I distinctly heard you call me a dummy," Kahner responded aloud. "Me, your own son!"

Inhaling and exhaling several times in quick succession Bastion pumped his fists at his sides becoming increasingly infuriated by the second.

"Yes," he said finally, pointing at Kahner. Then he turned toward Ariana. "No, and yes."

Ariana blinked. "Wait, was that a yes to being able to read minds or a yes to..."

"*Oh, for the love!*" About to explode Bastion fumed from the living room.

Chapter 16

Kalabernus is going "hunting?"

Uh, oh.

I'm thinking the "care package" the stalker left for them was probably not one of his best ideas. What do you think? Would you want a six foot eight-inch brute of a man who's tortured by demonic shadows hunting you? I know I sure wouldn't. Or would I?

Maybe I, Vortigern Black, am Kalabernus.

Could it be?

Wouldn't you love to know?

But seriously folks, it's times like these that I often wonder how people like this stalker of Ariana's get to be the way they are. Because, really, what kind of sick, twisted, demented sort of individual sends a baby doll filled with bloody animal parts to someone anyway?

Sheesh, disgusting!

Some people are just too messed up for words. One thing's for sure, this stalker of Ariana's is dangerous. Even more so now than he was before because it's entirely likely that he is now aware of what the RavenCroft family is capable of. That knowledge alone in the stalker's hands could spell disaster for the whole family.

And speaking of the RavenCroft's, they're just full of surprises, aren't they? Who would have guessed they knew sign language? That sure came in handy. After all, when you find your house is being bugged and you're worried there could be cameras too, being able to talk back and forth with your hands... Can we say, bonus?

If I were Ariana – and you never know, I could be - I think I would be wondering who Bastion RavenCroft really was. I mean, why would he have so many cool gadgets lying around, to begin with? As far as she knew, Bastion owned and ran a horse ranch. But then why would the owner of a horse ranch keep audio jammers and bug detectors on hand? If you started with the first book in this series, then you know that Bastion used to work for the CIA at one point. It could be these items were left behind from his many years of service. Supposedly, he no longer had ties with them.

Supposedly.

But that's for another story.

Right now, Kalabernus is livid and spoiling for a fight. He's done being one step behind this guy at any given turn. After seeing the terrified expression on Ariana's face when they discovered the doll, he was now more determined than ever to catch the stalker and put him away for good. As far as Kalabernus was concerned, her pursuer had been tormenting her for far too long.

The sicko wasn't just messing with the woman he cared about. Oh, no. Now he was terrorizing the woman he was falling in love with, who was pregnant with his child, and who might well be his wife if he could manage to convince her. On top of that, the knowledge Ariana's stalker had managed to gain from bugging her could not only ruin him but potentially put his entire family at risk. There was no way he was going to allow anyone he loved to be victimized.

Everything Kalabernus had been doing up to that point had simply been practice, a way to prepare for what was to come. But now…now the real hunt was on. And the stalker? Well…

…he was his prey.

- - -

"How do you even know he's out there? The stalker could be back at the cabin."

Kalabernus shook his head. "He goes where she goes. We both know that."

"This is a really bad idea, Kal," Kahner had said, using the childhood nickname he rarely ever used anymore. His brother's concern had been obvious. His father's too.

"What would you do?"

"I'm just saying what needs to be said."

"Bad or not I'm going. I gotta catch him, Kahner. She won't be safe until I do. You know that."

The conversation with his brother had been repeating in his mind most of the night as he moved with stealth through the forest behind the RavenCroft ranch house. It hadn't taken him long to put together what he'd need. Kalabernus had had most of it ready for the last several days. He'd merely been anticipating it would go down at his cabin, not his father's horse ranch.

Though quite familiar with the woods, having grown up in them, Kalabernus was at a disadvantage in that he hadn't been hunting in this terrain in a long while. He suspected what with the baby doll being left on the front porch that the stalker had been investigating the woods for the past twenty-four hours easily.

Taking a few extra minutes to gain his bearing, he allowed his eyes to adjust to the darkening surroundings. The shadows were out in force and the excitement they were experiencing left them volatile and frightening even for him. Their presence made the nighttime appear darker than usual, even with the moon high above them.

Anxiety and fear built within him. Kalabernus knew the demons had planned this confrontation. He knew he and Ariana had likely been brought together just for this purpose; to see which would prevail, the stalker who welcomed the darkness or Kalabernus who fought them at every turn. Even if he managed to overtake the man who hunted the woman he loved, he knew he still might lose. Because to catch him, he had to let them in. The question was, would he lose himself to the shadows in the process?

Refusing to think about it any further he continued forward, his breathing shallow, almost non-existent as his narrowed gaze took in every little detail. He'd picked up the little sicko's trail several minutes before, but he wanted to be sure it was a real trail and not a trap. The little bugger was irritatingly good at those and he'd nearly fallen for two of them within the past half hour.

His soft moccasins padded silently forward then he crouched, quickly scanning the brush filled ground before him.

Nothing.

How was that possible?

Doubling back to where he'd last saw the trail he touched his cold hand to the broken twig and leaf before him. The indentation was different. Shadows slithered around him, circling him like a curtain, enshrouding him.

"Lose him again, did we?" Veranke wheezed.

"Gonna lose, need to choose," Zalman crooned, his glowing red eye flashed as if he'd blinked. Kalabernus stared into the demons frightening visage, willing his stomach to keep from vomiting from the sickening sensation churning in his gut. There were so many of them; so many unfamiliar to him. They all taunted him, chanting in a language long lost to man.

"Where?" Kalabernus breathed, his voice barely audible above the quiet din of the forest. "Show me."

"Show you we can," Fallen oozed, his oily evil presence pressing closer still. It's tentacle-like essence twisted and turned around him, before him, above him.

"If within you, we were," Zalman connived.

A cool sweat beaded on Kalabernus's brow. Wiping it away, his gaze shifted uneasily about the forest. He turned on the spot, suddenly feeling as though he'd been led astray. The overwhelming sensation that he'd just been duped hit him full force. He didn't know how, but somehow, he just knew Ariana was in even more danger now than ever before.

Glancing behind him, he took a close look at the trail he'd been following then peered back in the direction he'd been heading. Fear laced within his chest, choking him, strangling him with the sudden knowledge of what he'd just allowed to happen.

"Ariana, no!"

The shadows coalesced, swaying above and around him, jeering at his stupidity. They knew, had known since he'd begun the trail. Ariana's stalker had been leading him away from the ranch house and toward the cabin – away from her. With every false trail he'd discovered, the stalker had been directing him further away. How could he have been so stupid?

Sneering angrily, he growled deep within his throat, pounding his fist into the nearest tree trunk. Unconcerned by the blood dripping from his knuckles nor the splintering whole in the tree, he turned and retreated hastily back toward the house. He'd have to start all over again and that was only if he wasn't already too late.

His feet flew across the forest floor, creating a trail of his own.

It was time.

He had no choice.

Dear God, help me save her in exchange for my soul.

The shadows chattered with excitement, floating along above him. The most troublesome three began circling him as he ran, their voluminous essences seemingly carrying him along, lifting him up from the ground. A feeling of weightlessness overcame him, his body propelling forward at a speed he didn't know he had.

"*Yield!*" Veranke shouted next to him.

Kalabernus whimpered, a sound unfamiliar to his ears. Terror gripped him at the thought of what he was about to allow.

"Do you yield!" Zalman shrieked to his right.

Head jerking toward the snarling monstrous demon Kalabernus cried out with fright. What normally appeared as a greenish black cloudy inky essence had now been replaced with a dragon-like bat-winged creature with a scaly hide. The moon glistened across its wings and back, its pronged tail trailing out behind. For the first time in his life, Kalabernus realized he was seeing the shadows in their truest form and the sight was terrifying. The forest was filled with them, surrounding him. Stumbling as he ran, they lifted him from the ground. He screamed in desperation.

"Ariana!"

A sense of foreboding overcame him as tears swam in his eyes. He was unsure which terrified him more at that moment. Losing her or losing his soul to these monstrous demons. Gritting his teeth, he firmly set his jaw and continued to run, insisting his feet touch the ground. Feeling the moccasins pushing once again back into the ground as he ran, he barreled forward around the bunch of trees near the first corral and barn. He could hear the horse within neigh in fright, sensing the presence of the shadows.

The backyard came into view, the sight befalling him instilling further terror within. The stalker already had her, and he was too far away.

"Do...you...yield?" Fallen bellowed with an evil grin, satisfaction clear in its glowing red eyes.

"Yes!"

- - -

Stupid.

She'd been so stupid.

Unable to sleep she'd come down for a glass of water. Seeing a large dark figure stumbling around in the yard she'd presumed it was Kalabernus upon seeing the coat the figure wore. Calling out to him he hadn't responded back, and she'd become afraid. Had he been hurt? Had her stalker shot him? Could he not speak?

The figure fell to the ground and was still.

Ariana had flung open the patio door and rushed out to him, her oversized white t-shirt billowing out about her as she ran.

"Kalabernus! Baby are you okay?"

Within a few feet of him, the man staggered back to his feet. She could see blood trickling down his pant leg and on his hands. Ripping off the black mask he wore the man's face twisted with an evil sneer as he snarled at her.

"Kalabernus?" he shouted angrily. Reaching for her, he snatched her arm tightly within his grasp, forcing her to the ground as she slipped in the grass and fell. "Baby?" he sneered. "He is nothing. *I* am everything. *You belong to me,*" he roared.

Screaming like a banshee, Ariana struggled to get from his painful grasp. Though smaller than Kalabernus by a good eight inches in height and size, he was still a pretty big man and he was strong – very strong.

Terror filled her at the thought something had happened to Kalabernus. Where was he? Why wasn't he here?

Fighting against her stalker who was attempting to drag her away from the house she screamed at him.

"Where is he? What did you do to him?" she yelled, her throat constricting with fear causing her voice to falter. She sobbed. Ariana didn't understand. She didn't even recognize the man before her and she had always thought she would. That she would have known him from some point in her life. But he was nobody to her.

"Where is *he*?" the man jeered. "He's dead for all we care. You would choose a vile creature such as he? A monster who sees demons over *me*?" The man shrieked angrily. His grip grew tighter. "No worries, Ariana. I know you've been deceived. I know you only want me. Don't you worry, Honey, we'll take care of that freak of nature inside you. I'll cut it out myself."

Taking hold of her with his other hand he lifted her, attempting to pull her over his shoulder but she'd have none of it.

"No! No!" Ariana screamed, banging at him with her fists and kicking at his shins.

Her stalker yelped in pain, releasing her with one hand as he bent to tend his wound. Things were not going as he'd planned. He'd managed to get the freak away from the house, but he'd run into one of his own traps, having forgotten where he'd set them all. Normally he was much more organized but, learning what he had of the RavenCroft family the night before, he'd had to speed things up and he'd been lax.

Fuming from being kicked in his sore leg he struck her, knocking her to the ground. Dazed and a bit disoriented she was much easier to manage in this state. The man lifted her from the ground, flinging her over his shoulder. Grunting in pain he turned about, watching where he stepped with his injured leg and began heading back toward the woods. His truck wasn't too far. He should be able to get to it quickly, even with the injury.

A keening howl erupted from the woods. The man's gaze fixed on the terrifying figure charging toward him in a rage. The haunting pale blue eyes glowed within the contorting features of Kalabernus's face.

The stalker swore. He'd never gotten this close. Dumping the woman unceremoniously on the ground, Anthony Warren flung his arms across his body defensively mere seconds before he was pummeled to the ground.

Head still a bit foggy, Ariana watched in horror as Kalabernus punched the man in the gut. Rearing back as the man huddled in a fetal position, he struck him again in the face. His fists flew, each one barreling into the man on the ground, inflicting increasingly heavy blows with each punch. Grabbing the man's wrist, he twisted it painfully causing it to snap and break.

"Kalabernus, wait!" Ariana called blinking back the fog. She lifted from the ground, her body shaking from being struck and from fear of the sight before her. The shadows were everywhere but they weren't shadows anymore. They had taken on a terrifying form she'd never seen. Screaming, shrieking and nearly peeing from fright, she cowered where she lay. She was desperate to get away from the creatures hovering around Kalabernus who were egging him on. They circled him, taunting him as they instructed him to kill, to murder, to rid the earth of the man who'd dare take what was his.

"Kalabernus," she cried, desperate to get his attention; to get him to stop.

He turned toward her then, his eyes gleaming with an unnatural light. His beautiful face twisted, and he snarled at her in a rage.

"That's right. It's *her* fault," Zalman screeched "Blame her."

"*Kill her!*"

"Dead. She needs to be dead!"

"And the baby with her."

The demonic shadows flew around him as Kalabernus stood rooted to the spot, the thought of murder in his mind. Kill, to kill. That's what he'd been born for. It's what he was good for. He was inherently evil after all. Or so he believed.

They cackled in their triumph, their knowing evil red eyes darting between the two as Kalabernus massive form slowly prowled toward her like a hunter to its prey.

"Kill her?" came an unnatural voice from deep within; a voice sounding nothing like him.

Ariana froze with fear. The gentle, caring man she knew as Kalabernus was no longer there. Something had taken a hold of him and she feared she knew what it was.

"Kalabernus, please," she begged while attempting to inch away from him unsuccessfully. His beefy hands reached out and grabbed her wrists. "Don't listen to them. They are evil. Remember? But you are not. Baby, please, you were born in love. And you love me, you said so yourself. True love could never hurt me."

Tears streamed down her face as she attempted to wriggle her wrist from his grasp. She needed only one. She needed to pull her treasure from its hiding spot at her hip. But his hold was too strong, and he wouldn't let go.

"I ... I love you?" Kalabernus snarled. Body tensing, his muscles clenched, and his face contorted. It was as though he were fighting an internal battle from which he was quickly losing.

"Yes, you love me. I know you do." Ariana cried as she wept. The cold was becoming too much. It seeped within her as though the shadows themselves were attempting to invade. "No!" She yelled angrily. Why must it be in her hand, she suddenly thought? Why not just believe, have faith, and repeat what she'd been taught so long ago by her sister?

"One day, you won't even need it, Ariana," her sister had said. *"One day hope will be within you and you'll believe without needing a talisman to remind you."*

In her tears, Ariana whispered fervently what her sister had taught her so long ago. "Those who seek the light of man shall find the light. Those who seek the light shall find protection. Those who seek the light shall find relief from their darkest pain. Those who seek the light shall find everlasting peace. *The light shines in the darkness and the darkness has not overcome it. Nor shall it ever."

Kalabernus roared, whether in anger, pain, or fear she was unsure. The deep guttural cry resonated throughout the ranch house and grounds even as he reared back as though to strike her.

*John 1:5

Chapter 17

Bastion could see it all in his head.

Coming out of his study he'd been heading down the hall towards his bedroom when it happened. An ominous feeling gripped him causing him to reach out to the hallway wall for support. The air around him shifted and spun as though he were walking through a hazy dream. Panic surged within him at the vision before him and the sight of Ariana outside the safety and security of his ranch home in the middle of the night. He could see the figure strike her and she fell. Yanking her up from the soft earth, the stalker pulled her over his shoulder and turned toward the forest in time to see Kalabernus charging him.

"No," Bastion choked out. Normally he couldn't see the shadows but sometimes while having a vision, he could often see what his son did. The sight of the demons which plagued him, having taken their true form, terrified him and he knew what that meant. Unable to break free of the vision until what he was being given was complete, he couldn't move to do anything to stop what was happening.

He could see Ariana tumble to the ground as the stalker attempted to flee. Bastion gagged, choking on the tears filling his eyes, nose and the back of his throat. The book he held in his hands fell to the floor with a soft thud. He leaned against the wall, frozen in place, helpless.

He watched in terror as Kalabernus beat the man into the ground, breaking his left wrist. He could see the shadows taunt him, convincing him to murder the helpless woman and his child laying nearby.

"No. Son, no," Bastion choked out, desperately attempting to move his legs down the hall.

If he could just get turned around.

Horrified he watched as his son lunged toward Ariana, gripping her roughly. The vision broke suddenly.

"No!" Bastion sobbed. Stumbling back down the hallway he raced to the fireplace. Yanking the thirty-thirty Winchester rifle from above the mantle he leaped over the chair, charged through the kitchen door and skidded to a halt near the open patio door.

Raising the rifle, he shot from memory, hoping desperately he'd hit his mark before it was too late. The deafening sound of a rifle blast resounded within the kitchen, as the air filled with the strong smell of gunpowder.

Pitching forward Kalabernus sprawled across Ariana, the weight of his body crushing her to the ground.

"Forgive me," Bastion choked out. Keeping his gun raised and ready in case another shot was required, he stood intently watching the scene before him, terrified he might have to shoot again.

The echoing sounds of feet pummeling down the stairwell didn't detract him from what he had to do. His shrewd gaze never wavering, Bastion watched anxiously as Kalabernus struggled up from his prone position. He appeared confused, disoriented and in pain.

"Dad! What in the world is going on?" Kahner hollered, running into the kitchen, his Glock at the ready.

"Don't move." Bastion's tone was deathly quiet.

Kahner stayed back but peered out at the sight before him.

"Kal!"

From his vantage in the yard, Kalabernus lifted his head slowly, peering up toward the kitchen patio. He could see his father standing with a shotgun in hand, and he could tell he was poised and ready to use it again if need be.

Dumbfounded and a bit disoriented, he glanced back over his shoulder and saw the lifeless prone form of Ariana's stalker, not even two feet away from him, with a knife lying limply in his grasp.

Anger and fear surged through Kalabernus at how close he'd come to getting killed and getting the woman he loved killed as well. Hearing her whispering fervently below him, he realized he still had her pinned where she couldn't directly get up.

"Kill her," screeched Zalman angrily at his side. "You must kill her!"

"No. I'll *never* hurt her."

"Why? *Stupid human*," Veranke growled in a violent rage. The 'troublesome three' had retaken their shadowy forms and now floated restlessly before him near Ariana's head.

"Because you want me to so badly," he ground out, shooting them a dark look that would have terrified them had they been a human man. "And because I love her. Stupid shadows. Who do you think was playing who here?"

The 'troublesome three' shrieked in unison, howling in their rage as they fled. The bright warm light, which had come the instant Ariana had begun whispering her prayer, began growing in strength and size preventing them from tarrying longer.

"Are you okay? Please tell me. I didn't hurt you, did I?"

"No. I'm okay, just frightened."

The shadows were receding, no longer interested in a game that had ended badly, as far as they were concerned.

"That's understandable considering what you've just been through." Adjusting his position, he scooped her into his arms and carried her toward the house, ignoring his own aches and pains. His chest heaved from the exertion it had taken to get to Ariana in time, but he was starting to regain his composure. Relieved to be holding her safely in his arms he beamed down at her tenderly then back over at his dad.

He scowled as he came closer to the patio and shouted at his father. "Do you intend to shoot me, or what?"

"I'm still thinking about it," Bastion growled, holding the rifle at the ready. "Don't you *ever* do that to me again," he demanded roughly, finally relaxing his posture. Resting the barrel of the gun on the kitchen floor he leaned on it slightly as though in need of support.

Though he was trying to hide it Kalabernus could see the fear in his father's eyes. The thought of having to shoot his own son had terrified him.

"You were supposed to shoot me if I got too close to her," Kalabernus said irately, though clearly grateful he hadn't.

"I was trying. The other guy just got in the way," Bastion insisted with an amused glint. "I suppose we best be calling Sheriff RavenCroft and his deputies out here. They'll want to be getting in the middle of this, I imagine."

"I'm sure they will," Kahner said with relief next to him. He'd never been so grateful in his life that his father had once been a sniper in the armed services than in that moment.

Ducking as he strolled into the kitchen Kalabernus continued toward the stairs.

"Where do you think you're going?" Kahner hollered crossly at his brother.

"Up to bed of course."

"Now?"

"Well, yeah. I hear sex after an intense life-threatening situation can be extremely good. I intend to find out."

Gasping, Ariana's shocked gaze flitted toward his father and brother. Covering her mouth with one hand she giggled into his shoulder. She didn't argue but she hadn't yet agreed either. Her eyes sparkled with amusement.

"Kalabernus, you git! Don't you think you should make sure she's okay first?" Bastion asked crossly.

"Oh, right," he responded, appearing properly chastised. "Ariana, Honey. Are you all right? I mean, do you think we'd be okay if…"

Smiling Ariana leaned forward, wrapped her arms around his neck and kissed him. He shivered, a sound of pleasure escaping him as he groaned into her mouth. He responded with an elated shout. "Oh, yeah! Call me when Kalturek gets here. That should give us fifteen minutes or so," he said heading up the stairs.

"In that case, give us a five-minute head start. Then call," Ariana yelled down the stairwell as they disappeared from view. She laughed, the genuine sound free of the tension and stress she had been experiencing for longer than she could remember. Would she let him, she wondered? It was a delicious notion either way.

"Oh, good grief," Bastion vented angrily, rolling his eyes.

"Is everything okay down here?" Sable asked tentatively. Coming into the kitchen from the entrance hallway she missed seeing Kalabernus and Ariana exit upstairs.

"Yeah, Honey. It's over. Dad got the guy stalking Ariana. We're about to call the Sheriff." Kahner quickly turned his wife about so she couldn't see the body in the yard.

"Oh, dear. Okay." Sable was just grateful everything was all right. Catching sight of the book lying on the floor she reached down and picked it up. "Huh, that's odd. I thought I left that upstairs in our bedroom."

"Probably just dropped it on your way. Here, I'll take it up for you," Bastion said quickly, taking it from her hand while walking swiftly past her to the stairwell.

"Uh, Dad?" Kahner called, forcing his father to turn around.

Bastion stared as though waiting for something else to happen. "Yes?" he prompted.

"The rifle? You're taking it with you?"

"Yup," Bastion quipped. Lifting the rifle, he looked at it then back at Kahner with a mischievous glint in his eye. "Thinking I might shoot that son of mine anyway," he said finally, then disappeared.

Epilogue

What?

You didn't honestly think Bastion was going to shoot his own son, did you? If he had that wouldn't have made for a good story. Course, just because he isn't going to shoot him, doesn't mean he won't threaten him a bit.

It's always nice to see a happy ending. Don't you think?

And in case you all are wondering, Bastion was thinking he might well shoot Kalabernus anyway for two very different reasons.

First, because his son was taking Ariana upstairs, so he could make a little love to her. But they weren't married yet. Bastion fully understood human nature, of course, but he also believed in the importance of marriage. He did have some scruples, after all, and he'd thought he'd taught his son better than that too. He fully intended to stop him before things got X-rated. As far as he was concerned, if they were going to be a couple and have babies, then they needed to be married. This might seem a bit backward to you, considering she's pregnant already, but just because someone makes a bad choice initially, doesn't mean they can't put effort into making things right.

Bastion's second reason was that he firmly believed no man or woman should ever willingly invite the darkness into their life if they have a choice, no matter what the circumstances. To do so was just asking for 'Trouble,' because there was often an adverse rippling effect from such decisions no one could ever possibly foresee. Kalabernus had clearly broken his promise and allowed the shadows to take him over. That notion riled him just about as much as the fact that his son intended to consummate his marriage before the wedding even took place.

Shoot, the man hadn't even proposed to her yet!

The RavenCroft patriarch might not have been raised in a house of faith but he figured no good ever came from letting the shadows in. He'd seen proof of that first hand...and paid a rather high price for it too. But that's another story.

In case you're wondering who that stalker was, Sheriff Kalturek RavenCroft managed to get the prints off the body of the stalker and soon learned that the man's name had been Anthony Warren. After a little investigation, it was discovered that the man had been a classmate of Ariana's sister. This knowledge prompted her to dig back into her sister's things and that's when she found Sareena's diary.

According to what her sister wrote, Anthony Warren had developed an unhealthy fixation on Ariana at an early age. Sareena had initially thought it just a school-boy crush that would eventually go away after a couple years. But then she caught Anthony following her sister around and, on several occasions, peeking through her bedroom window at night. That was when she made the mistake of confronting Anthony instead of telling her parents. She threatened to tell on him if he didn't stop. Unfortunately, Sareena had no idea how truly dangerous young Anthony Warren really was. She never got a chance to tell anybody about her concerns because the day after her last entry in her diary, she died in a car accident when her supposedly frayed brake lines went out on her. She was sixteen at the time.

Though Sheriff RavenCroft couldn't prove that Anthony Warren had anything to do with Sareena Davis's accident many years before, between the timing of her last diary entry and what Bastion saw in his vision from several days prior, it led them to believe that he was likely responsible for Sareena's death.

Man, it broke Ariana's heart to find this out. Her sister had tried to protect her and wound up dead for her efforts.

Fortunately, she didn't stay sad for long. Not wanting to take anything for granted where Ariana was concerned, Kalabernus pulled her into the living room the next Wednesday night, bent down on one knee in front of the roaring fire in his father's hearth, and asked Miss Ariana Davis to marry him. His resounding whoop upon hearing her say yes could be heard fifty yards away down near the stables by the ranch hands.

It helped that the living room windows happened to be propped open at the time. Which makes no sense to me seeing as it was November and there was a fire going in the fireplace. But then no one ever said the RavenCroft's weren't a bit different.

That's it for now.

You'll have to wait to find out what happens next because this story isn't anywhere near over yet. There's so much more going on than what you might realize. For the shadows might have been 'Trumped' this time in their efforts to create havoc and chaos with all their 'Terrible' tactics but they weren't done yet. They were already regrouping and forming another plan. And they had already found their next mark.

As for who I, Vortigern Black, am? Well, let me ask you... Do you have any ideas yet? Have you at least narrowed it down to whether I am male or female?

Hahahahaha!

I bet right now, you're presuming that Vortigern Black is a male, aren't you? How sexist is that? Just because the name seems masculine doesn't mean I'm a guy. After all, Bastion RavenCroft himself re-named his own son, Toni Starck, now didn't he? When he did that he spelled it with an 'I.' Typically, that would be the effeminate way of spelling the name.

I suppose you're probably thinking, "Shoot, can't prove it by me. The image on the cover of the last book and this one has been a guy. That has to mean you're one of the men in the RavenCroft tale."

Nope.

Not necessarily.

Geez, people, haven't you ever heard of an avatar before?

Hahahahaha!

In case you haven't, an avatar - as in the circumstance we're using here - is an icon or figure representing a person in computer games, internet forums, and in other areas. For this series, I have chosen one for me to protect my identity. Hence the picture on the book cover. Because, you know...

...I'm deep, deep undercover after all.

And as for that hint, I promised you...

...gather your suspect list already and try and keep up. I know it's hard but I'm confident you can do it.

I will tell you this much... In this story alone, there were six new characters. If you check the character list at the back of this book, you'll see it's true. That's a lot of new potential suspects, don't you think? Allow me to save you some 'Trouble.'

I, Vortigern Black, am not any of the new characters introduced in this book.

Be seeing you soon.

A Note From the Author

Thank you for taking the time to read my story. I truly hope you enjoyed it. And if you wouldn't mind... Please be sure to leave a review of Karisma Trouble at amazon.com. I'd love to hear from you!

I'd also like to welcome you to experience...

Total Kayos
An Unfortunate Lineage
Volume IV

OR, if you're disinclined toward reading faith-based fiction at this time, (and there is nothing wrong with that, of course) you may skip on to...

Deadly Karisma
An Unfortunate Lineage Finale
Volume V

OR, if you're ready to skip to the finale then feel free to skip over everything and go straight to it.

Karisma Kayos: Out of Time
An Unfortunate Lineage Finale
Volume VII

Either way, I hope you're enjoying the series so far!

Delaine Christine

CHARACTER LIST OF SUSPECTS

Vortigern Black - Narrator of the RavenCroft story and a character within. But which one of the following characters lays claim to the pseudonym?

Sareena Davis (?) - Heroine of this story, she is single without children, and originally from Dalton Massachusetts. (? - Or, is that really who she is?)

Angela Powers - Old college roommate and good friend of Sareena Davis.

Heaton Jones - On again, off again boyfriend of Angela Powers.

Avery Shenanigan - Bartender at Shenanigans and little-known owner of said business. But now *you* know. Can you keep a secret?

Kami Russell - Old roommate of Sareena Davis's in Dalton Massachusetts.

Stalker - Not going to tell you who this sick, twisted individual is just yet. You'll find out in the end.

Bastion RavenCroft - Patriarch of the RavenCroft clan and father of the following from eldest to youngest. Triplets: Kahner, Kalturek, Kalabernus. Fraternal twins: Drayke and Mackenzie. And last but not least, the baby of the family, Synedra.

Kahner RavenCroft aka Toni Starck - Firstborn of triplets, he is now married to Sable RavenCroft.

Sable RavenCroft aka Kalysta Radford - New wife of Kahner RavenCroft. She was formerly married to drug kingpin Lionel Radford for over ten years. She is the mother of Lisa (10), and fraternal twins Adam (7), and Jordon RavenCroft/Radford (7).

Eliza RavenCroft - Former wife of Kahner RavenCroft from fourteen years prior.

Kalturek RavenCroft - The Second-born of triplets, he is married to Stephanie RavenCroft.

Stephanie RavenCroft - Wife of Kalturek RavenCroft, she desperately wants a gifted child.

Kalabernus RavenCroft - Third born of triplets, he is single and a recluse because of his gift.

Drayke RavenCroft – Mackenzie's fraternal twin and fourth born, he is married to Laynie RavenCroft.

Laynie RavenCroft - Wife of Drayke RavenCroft, she also wants children, but it doesn't matter whether they are gifted or not.

Mackenzie Funnie (RavenCroft) – Drayke's fraternal twin and fifth born, she is married to Dr S.T. Funnie.

Dr S.T. Funnie - He is the husband of Mackenzie Funnie (RavenCroft).

Synedra Kayme (RavenCroft) - Sixth born and the baby of the family, she is married to Nathan Kayme.

Nathan Kayme - He is the husband of Synedra Kayme (RavenCroft), he is a private investigator.

Agent Ricardo Pegueros - He works for the Central Intelligence Agency (CIA) in undercover operations, specializing in information retrieval.

Lionel Radford - Younger brother to Kobi Radford, he and his brother are drug cartel kingpins with brutal tempers. Lionel is married to Kalysta Radford and is the father of Lisa (10), Adam (7), and Jordan Radford (7).

Kobi Radford - Older brother of Lionel Radford. He heads the drug cartel left to them by their father.

Photo by Rosemary MacDaniel

Author Delaine Christine

Who is she really?
One more guess from within
She is a part of the story once again.
An author of fiction who writes what she knows
She might well have more than one name to disclose
Inspiring imagination between two worlds
This author finds she must overcome many hurdles
So more than one name she goes by in her life:
author Vortigern Black, mother, chef and wife.

For more about the series
and the author

vortigernblack.com

smashwords.com/profile/view
/DelaineChristine

Or to Contact the Author:
delainechristine15@gmail.com